Mandy and the Pharaohs

DORA CAMPBELL

For Colleen who, thank God, is nothing like Mandy's sister.

One

Two blokes booked appointments with me that Tuesday, and both of them asked me for a drink.

The day began badly enough. I arrived at Luxor only to find that both juniors, Rose and Emmy, had called in sick.

"That's the third time in two weeks!" I exclaimed, slamming my silver drawstring bucket bag onto the desk.

Robbie raised one delicately arched eyebrow. "Don't shoot the messenger, Mandy darlin'. And that's not wholly accurate. Emmy's called in four times in the past fortnight."

"You're right. I shouldn't lump Rose with her, poor girl. Rose never calls in unless something's really the matter."

"Neither does Emmy. She may be suffering from the worst hangover she's had this week."

I sighed. "I'll have to have it out with her, eventually. But what are we going to do now with both juniors out?"

Both of Robbie's eyebrows rose. Today, he'd outlined his left eye with black eyeliner and garnished it with thick mascara. "Well, the punters will have to survive without Rose and Emmy oohing and aahing."

"I know that! But who's going to answer the phone if we're both with clients?"

"It'll work, darlin'."

And suddenly, I knew that we would make it work. We'd answer the phone, sweep the floor, make tea, and do everything we needed to do to ensure that the salon ran smoothly.

"If it does, it's because of you," I said.

A smile spread over Robbie's face, and despite his spiky red hair and eyeliner, he looked like a boy. He was only twenty after all although he'd been working in London for three years.

I didn't know too much about Robbie's early life. At seventeen, he'd left Belfast not so much to escape the Troubles as the troubles at home. When he was eight, his dad had come home to find Robbie applying his older sister's eyeliner. He'd been copying Marc Bolan. That time, he got away with a welt on his bum. Nine years later, when he'd made himself up like Boy George, his dad had blackened his right eye and broken his left arm.

Quickly, Robbie recovered himself. "We've got no choice," he said airily.

"Well, let's look at the day, then."

The diary was full. Robbie's customers were all repeats. I recognized all but two of the names on my list.

"That's funny; they're both blokes," I said. Although Luxor was a unisex salon, almost all of our clients were female.

A Jack Slayton had scheduled a haircut at eleven. Then my last appointment at half-four was with a David Davies.

"David Davies," I muttered. "Why do I know that name?"

"You're bound to remember a Welshman with a name like that."

I shook my head. "I don't know that many Welshmen, and I can't remember one with that name."

"Luxor made the *Evening Standard* last Thursday," said Robbie. "That brought in a few punters. Rose and Emmy were off their heads scheduling appointments on Friday and Saturday. It's probably some fat little man from Swansea who wants to gawk at you."

"Well, any publicity is good publicity, I suppose," I said, laughing. "Even if they just want to see the drummer's ex-wife."

It was the first time the press had mentioned Luxor since I'd opened the salon a year earlier. The article was about how the ex-wife of a once top drummer had a salon off the King's Road. Of course, I wished it had been about the quality of our work or the ambiance of the salon, but beggars couldn't be choosers. At least, the journalist had mentioned the Egyptian-themed décor and included a rather flattering photo of me.

I didn't have time to speculate about my clients or anything else for the next two hours. Somehow, I managed to do two haircuts, a permanent, and a frost and cut while acting as my own junior. I swept up the punters' hair while asking about their holidays—were they going anywhere that winter—and made tea for Robbie's clients while answering the phone. The old me would have needed several fags and biscuits to see herself through a morning like this, but I made it without either.

Still, I would have to sack Emmy if this continued. If only she didn't look fifteen instead of nineteen.

I removed the cape from Nancy, my ten o'clock.

Her eyes met mine in the mirror. "How do I look?" she asked.

At thirty, she was four years younger than I was, but worried about getting older. This was because nothing in her life had gone the way she had wanted it to. Although she'd been a secretary at an advertising agency for eight years, she had an English degree and longed to be a copywriter. A year ago, her boyfriend had left her for a twenty-one-year-old.

"Like an attractive professional woman," I said. "The short blonde hair makes you look like Princess Di—if she had to work for a living."

Nancy's mouth broke into a smile, and the pinched look left her face. Suddenly, she looked prettier and more capable. She held her head a little higher as I escorted her to the front of the salon.

At the front desk, Robbie lifted one eyebrow. "Your eleven o'clock's here."

Only one man sat in the waiting area. As I approached, he rose from his seat. He looked about fifty, and his light brown hair was grey around the temples. Though he was only of medium height and build and wore a plain grey suit, he exuded confidence. It somehow seemed appropriate that he sat beneath the mural of the pharaohs with their jeweled headdresses.

What a silly thought. I shoved it aside.

I smiled and extended my hand.

"Mr. Slayton? I'm Mandy Wilt. Give us a minute to clean this up, and then I'll take you back."

His handshake was firm, and so were the blue eyes that met mine beneath the high forehead. "Well met, and of course," he said in a Scots voice.

I swept Nancy's hair as quickly as I could. Of all the bloody days for Rose and Emmy to call in.

Once again, Jack Slayton stood when I approached.

"Thanks so much for your patience, Mr. Slayton. Do come back."

He followed me past the paintings of Egyptian gods and goddesses that lined the gold wall behind our stations. There was Anubis with his dog head; Bastet who appeared half woman, half-cat; Horus with his falcon head; and others whose names I was always forgetting.

"So you're from Scotland, then," I said as my fingers worked in the warm sudsy water.

"Glasgow born and bred. Was it that obvious?"

"Just a bit. Have you been in London long?"

"Two years."

I couldn't ask a client why he was in London, but I asked him the next best question. "How do you like it thus far?"

"There's opportunity here for those who aren't afraid to get their hands dirty," he declared over the whoosh of water.

"And lots of fun for those who want it."

"That, too."

As I led him to my station, I was oddly glad that I hadn't had to entrust the shampooing to Rose or Emmy.

"What sort of cut are you looking for today?" I asked as he sat in my chair. His hair had been cut quite recently by the look of it.

"Oh, just a trim."

A very slim trim. I took a comb and razor from the vanity.

He gestured at the figure with a falcon's head on the wall. "It's clever—the pharaohs and all."

"Thanks. A friend of a friend is an Egyptologist, so she set me straight on the gods and goddesses. That one's called Horus, I think."

"I meant the idea itself, a salon with an Egyptian theme."

I parted his hair with the comb and made a careful cut. "I wanted something a bit different."

"Stand out from the competition. Well, it worked. You've got the press taking notice."

I smiled. Robbie was right. "You saw us in the *Evening Standard,* then?"

"I did. And I thought the Egyptian theme was unique. It suggests luxury, and people don't despise that nowadays."

"I'm glad you like it."

"But I must confess I didn't come just to see paintings of pharaohs."

My eyes met his in the mirror. His were a steelier blue than my ex-husband's, and their gaze held mine.

"I came to meet the proprietor."

My mouth fell open in a smile, revealing the gap between my front teeth. Seeing my reflection, I decided that maybe I wasn't on the brink of middle age after all.

"Can I have dinner with you tonight?"

Even my ex-husband hadn't moved that quickly.

"I'd love to, but I've got to pick up my kids after work."

"How about a drink, then? In the Chelsea Potter Pub just around the corner?"

"I could meet you at five." I should be done with the Welshman by then, and in a pinch, Robbie could always finish him off.

"At five, then. In the Chelsea Potter." Jack smiled, and the lines around his eyes made him appear distinguished.

The afternoon was as chaotic as the morning, but I was buoyed along by the thought of the drink. I'd seen a few men since my divorce became final five years earlier, but nothing serious—that is, nothing that had lasted. And I'd been so busy with work and the kids and then opening Luxor that there hadn't been a lot of time for romance.

But this felt different.

At twenty-five past four, I saw off a client with her new permanent.

"Do you think the Welshman will show?" asked Robbie after she left.

"Who knows, love? Be careful, or I might foist him on you."

As I swept my station, I heard the door open. I wouldn't look just yet. Robbie greeted the client and offered him tea. Then he was beside me.

"Not fat and definitely not Welsh," he whispered. "Not the accent anyhow."

I would have to do something about his habit of commenting on clients when they were in the salon. But not today.

I made my way to the waiting area. A newspaper hid the punter's face. The *Evening Standard* had brought him in, and here he was hiding behind the *Guardian*.

"Good afternoon, Mr. Davies," I said.

The paper moved down, revealing a long face topped by short brown hair combed forward to a point and capped by a drooping mustache.

"Hi, Mandy," he said.

"Dave, what are you doing here?" I exclaimed.

I couldn't believe I was raising my voice at the salon. Thank God no one else was there except for Robbie and me. But I couldn't believe my ex-husband had booked a haircut with me.

He smiled sheepishly. "Getting a haircut?"

"I can see that. But I didn't know it was you."

"I used my mum's maiden name."

Now I remembered. Dave had grown up near Hastings, but his mother was Welsh.

It was the first time in five years we'd spoken face to face at such close quarters. We talked about the kids on the phone—perfectly amiably, thank you very much. When he picked them up for the weekend, I'd wave to him from the front door. I knew that styles had changed and that he hadn't had long hair since the late seventies. Still, it was a shock to see him with short hair—in my mind, he still sported the shoulder-length hair he'd had when we'd met almost thirteen years earlier.

"But why did you come here?" My voice was shrill, and I hated it.

Robbie, bless him, was sweeping invisible hair on the other side of the room though I knew he was taking in every bloody word.

"To see your place, I suppose. It looks great, Mandy. I'm proud of what you've done."

As though he had any right to be. My chin rose.

"Thank you. Now you've seen it."

Dave rose from his chair. "I'm looking forward to seeing the rest of it."

Smiling, he stepped toward me. He was as tall and loose-limbed as ever, and he smelled of soap and tobacco and himself as he always did. But there were lines around his light blue eyes that hadn't been there before, and there was a hesitation I didn't recognize either.

"And I thought we could get a drink afterward," he said.

"Why?" my voice quivered.

He paused. "Well, to talk, I suppose."

"If you want to talk about Sam or Katie, you can call me at home," I replied crisply.

"But I don't want to talk about them," he said.

"They're your children!"

He sighed. "I meant, not now. I just wanted to have a chat, I guess. I'd like to hear about your business, your life."

He thought he could just waltz into my life after we had been divorced for five years. And that divorce had come after six years of cheating and probably more because it had all started long before we were married. . .

I stood tall.

"As a matter of fact, I'm meeting someone for a drink," I said. "Robbie will look after you."

I held my head high as I grabbed my handbag and coat and sailed from the salon.

Two

I rounded the corner as quickly as I could and stepped into an alley. My chest heaved as I stared at the fag ends and chocolate wrappers on the pavement.

I couldn't believe Dave had had the cheek to book a haircut at Luxor—and to tell me how proud he was of my work. As soon as we were engaged, he'd been after me to stop working though I'd kept cutting hair a few days a week until Sam was on the way. Once we were married, he'd expected me to be the perfect wife: to cook, clean (though, of course, he'd paid for a cleaner), look after the kids, and spend his money.

He'd always been better at that than I was. And at controlling his temper.

Like that little exchange in the salon. Robbie had heard all of it.

Thank God Rose and Emmy had been out that day. And Robbie, bless him, had been there to take over. And above all, no other customers had been there for my outburst.

Taking a deep breath, I lifted my head. Raindrops bounced off the rubbish bin beside me; one glanced off my cheek. Most of the people passing to and fro toted umbrellas.

Mine was where I'd left it: on the kitchen table. The one day I had an assignation with an attractive man, I'd forgotten my bloody umbrella.

At least, the Chelsea Potter wasn't far. I could make a run for it and then adjust my makeup in the ladies before Jack arrived. I tucked my handbag under my arm and dashed out of the alley.

I ran, or trotted, really, down the street as that was all my heels would allow me to do. In quick succession, I said, "Excuse me, sorry," to a punk in a mohawk with a studded leather jacket, two girls with enormous dark perms, and a man with a briefcase.

The rain grew more intense as I turned onto the King's Road. I hoisted my handbag over my head—I didn't want my mascara to run and turn my face into a harlequin mask.

Just ahead of me, the Chelsea Potter's windows beckoned. I dashed toward the pub and threw open the door. Just then, my right leg gave out.

I pitched forward, grasping the doorknob.

A man and woman occupied the table near the window. Their eyes widened as I steadied myself on the door.

Perhaps I looked worse than I thought. I flashed a smile at them and sailed to the ladies.

The reflection in the gilt-edged mirror didn't look as wild-eyed as I'd feared. A few locks of hair had gone astray with the humidity. I soon set it to rights with a tiny tube of hair gel in my bag. A slick of red lipstick, and I was as good as new.

I grinned at my reflection as though we were two friends sharing a joke. Here I was, a salon owner, a mother of two, and I'd nearly fallen because I'd been running in heels. In London in the rain, no less.

It had been years since I'd run in heels. It was one of my early dates with Dave—it must have been 1972. We'd taken a walk in Richmond Park, and somehow, I'd gotten him to chase me. Of course, everything was platform heels then, so running in heels hadn't been quite as dangerous. . .

Now, after my near accident, I felt young again. Once more, I beamed at the mirror. Today, I was pleased with my dark blonde hair with its half-up, half-down tousled style, my boxy lime-green earrings, even the gap between my teeth.

Dave had always said I'd looked like a brown-eyed Pattie Boyd.

"If Pattie put on a stone and half," I'd said. And had grown up in Croydon, I might have added.

"Well, a few more puddings wouldn't hurt Mrs. Harrison's figure," Dave had replied, his hand resting on my bum.

For years, I'd scoffed when I recalled that conversation. Especially once I'd gained a few stone. But today, it didn't seem ridiculous that someone had once compared me to a famous model, the muse of a Beatle, and that a distinguished older man had just asked me for a drink.

I glanced at my watch. Ten till five. I didn't want to look as though I were waiting for Jack. But I didn't want to venture out into the rain and risk messing up my hair and makeup again. And if he had already arrived, leaving and coming back would only look ridiculous.

So I did the sensible thing: I left the ladies and looked for a table near the window, where I could wait for Jack.

A man in a grey suit occupied the table where the couple had been sitting earlier. He rose at my approach, and I recognized him as Jack.

"Hi, Mr. Slayton," I said.

"If you call me Jack, I promise not to call you Mrs. Wilt."

I laughed. "Agreed."

His lips were firm, but his steely blue eyes relaxed as they smiled into mine.

"In that case, Mandy, let's get a drink."

I knew the barman well as I often had a drink here with my staff after work. But if he was surprised to see me with a man, he gave no sign of it as he served Jack a gin and tonic and me a glass of chardonnay.

After Jack paid for our drinks, we returned to the small table near the window.

Jack lifted his glass. "Santé."

"Santé." Our glasses clinked.

"Do you come here often?" he asked.

I nodded. "Sometimes, I come here with my staff after work."

"How many people work for you?"

I wanted to giggle. It was a funny question for a first date—if this was indeed a date. But his blue eyes studied me carefully. He was serious.

"Three. One other stylist—Robbie, the one who greeted you. And two juniors. They both called in today."

"Happen often, does it?"

"Hardly ever with one girl. The other, bless her, manages to call in once or twice a week."

"That can't go on."

"I'll have it out with her sooner or later."

"Sooner."

The word sounded oddly decisive in his Scots accent. I laughed.

"What's so funny?" He sounded genuinely puzzled.

"You've just bought me a drink, and you're already giving me business advice."

This time, Jack laughed. "Blame my frugal Scots upbringing, but I don't like to see anyone taken advantage of. Especially someone who's worked so hard to build something so worthwhile."

He gazed intently at my face. "Thank you," I said and lowered my eyes.

I paused before adopting a lighter tone. "Now that you've given me advice, can I ask what your business is?"

"Of course. I'm a property developer. I buy old buildings, renovate them, and sell them."

So he was probably up to giving business advice. "Is that what you've always done?"

"For over twenty-five years now though there have been some other ventures here and there. I got my start in Glasgow and then did some work in Leeds and Bradford. I've been in London for two years, redoing some properties in Belsize Park and Hampstead."

"It sounds exciting."

"It is. You never quite know whether a place is going up or down, but you make an educated guess, and more often than not, you're right. And if not, you know how to be less wrong than the other man. Like you with your salon. Luxor."

"It's not like being a property developer. I'm a hairdresser. A stylist if you want to be posh."

"I don't. And you're more than a hairdresser: you're an entrepreneur. You had a clever idea, and you made a success of it."

Perhaps he'd gotten rich flattering his rivals.

I set my glass down on the table. "Look. I started doing hair full time again after my divorce five years ago. Just over a year ago, I saw a little salon for sale off the King's Road. I put in a bid, and I bought it. I thought it would be fun to give it an Egyptian theme. A friend of a friend—the Egyptologist I mentioned earlier—sorted out all the décor. An artist friend did all the paintings. It brought in a few new punters, and most of my clients from the last salon followed me to Luxor. I was lucky, that's all."

Jack shook his head. "You made your own luck, Mandy. You knew your trade, you saw something in the market, and you took a risk. No, you'll have to get used to being a success."

Maybe not, but I could get used to this sort of praise. "I'll work on it."

"You're already there."

I finished my wine.

"Would you like another drink?" asked Jack.

I shook my head. "I've got to fetch the kids from the neighbor's. But thanks for the drink; this has been lovely."

"How many children do you have?"

"Two. Sam's ten, and Katie's seven."

"That's quite a lot to take on, two bairns and a business."

"They make being a mum easy. When I look back, my sister and I were nightmares."

Now the blue eyes were amused. "I have trouble imagining you as a nightmare."

"But you don't know me very well."

"I'd like to. When can you have dinner with me?"

"Saturday. The kids will be with their dad this weekend."

"Excellent. Shall I meet you at Luxor or pick you up in—"

"Ealing. But I work Saturdays, so meeting me at Luxor is best."

"Shall we say six o'clock, then?"

"Yes."

"Good." His brow furrowed. "Is he reliable, this musician type? He will show up this weekend?"

Musician type. As though Dave were a teenager with a drum kit.

"He will. He's good with the kids, I'll say that for him."

"Glad to hear it." Jack gave a quick nod. "Would you like a lift to Ealing?"

"Thanks, but I drove today."

"Well, then, Mandy, till Saturday." He smiled as he pressed my hand, his fingers resting on mine a second longer than was strictly necessary.

My red Vauxhall Cavalier was parked two streets over. I might have looked like a giddy girl when I dashed to the pub, but I felt like a woman of the world as I strolled past pubs and restaurants, their lighted windows warm and inviting in the November dusk. The rain had ceased, Chelsea was beautiful at night, I was the proprietor of a successful salon, and in four days, I would have my first date in two years.

Three

"How was Mr. Davies?" I asked Robbie the next day. I felt sheepish about losing my temper in front of Robbie and passing Dave off on him.

Behind the desk, Robbie raised one arched eyebrow and shrugged. "Oh, Mr. Davies-Wilt was perfectly charming. I would have given him something more daring, but he was satisfied with a simple trim."

"So he was polite to you?"

"Of course, he was, darlin'. He might not have gotten the proprietress, but he made do with the second stylist."

"Glad to hear it," I said. Dave had occasionally made remarks about poofs when we were married although I didn't really think he'd be unkind to a boy cutting his hair.

"We got on like a house afire. We talked about music. His, mainly."

" I didn't know you liked Serval." I'd known Robbie for two years now—we'd worked together at my previous salon, and I'd hired him when I opened Luxor—and I was still learning new things about him.

"I wasn't a fanny-fan, darlin'. But I liked a couple tracks from their glam phase. I remember Greg and Alec in their eyeliner on *Top of the Pops*."

It was my turn to cock an eyebrow. "So Dave was safe."

"Sacred."

I laughed. "My friend Elsie—you know, Alec's wife—still shudders when she talks about Alec in eyeliner. She's American, you know."

Of course, I'd been relieved when the make-up phase, just a couple months in the summer of 1973, had ended and Dave had grown back his mustache in time for our wedding that autumn.

The front door swung open, and in rapid succession, Rose and Emmy tumbled through it.

From behind the desk, Robbie blinked at the juniors. "That was a rapid recovery," he said blandly.

Perhaps honey would work better than vinegar. "It's lovely to see both of you," I said.

Beneath her close-cropped curls, Rose's large brown eyes were apologetic as she set her handbag behind the desk. "I had an upset stomach," she said. "It was one of those twenty-four-hour things. Now my mum and sisters have it."

Rose and her large family lived in Notting Hill in the same flat her parents had occupied since they'd emigrated from Jamaica twenty years earlier. The family needed her income, and I knew she was serious about becoming a hairdresser.

Emmy nodded rapidly, her boxy yellow earrings bouncing amidst her crimped brown layers. "That's just how it was with me. I spent most of yesterday over the toilet, but today I'm right as rain. It must have been the same bug."

She flashed a particularly sweet smile as if to show me just how healthy she felt that morning. Last week, she'd reported two migraines as well as a bout of "woman trouble."

Robbie's smile grew even archer. "And in which club did you pick it up?" he murmured.

"Well, I'm relieved you're both on the mend," I said. "Now there's lots to do before the punters arrive." I'd have to have it out with Emmy some other time when we weren't so busy.

Between Luxor and home, I didn't have much time for thinking that week. There was simply too much to do between cutting hair, ordering supplies, getting the kids to school each morning, and cooking dinner or ordering takeaways at night. But on my morning commute, my mind wandered to my upcoming date. Since my divorce, I'd tried going out with three men, and none of them had stuck.

Soon after my divorce was final, Charlie had come into my life. We'd been at school together, and we'd met again at an old friend's birthday drinks. He'd always made me laugh at school, but then again, I was pretty easy to distract. I remembered how much fun he'd been, and with his red hair and stocky build, he was so different to Dave. When he'd asked me to dinner, I'd said yes without hesitation.

Our first couple dates were a good laugh. For a funny man, Charlie could be considerate, and even though he was on the dole and all he could afford were fish and chips or hamburgers, it was nice to be out with someone.

Then one day, he asked me for a loan. His gran would be turned out of her flat if he didn't help with the rent. I couldn't let that happen, so I handed over the money. The next week, he needed a couple hundred for his great-uncle.

That was the last of Charlie.

About six months later, a girl from work introduced me to Eddie when we were out for drinks. He was one of her mates' brothers, and he worked at a record shop. I was thirty and he was twenty-one, but I told myself age was just a number. And since I'd put on a few stone since I'd had the kids, it was reassuring I could still attract a younger man.

We went out for a drink on our own a few days later. We talked about music, and it turned out Eddie played drums. After Ian Paice from Deep Purple, Dave was his favorite drummer. He'd been listening to Serval and trying to copy Dave's licks since he was fourteen. Was there any way I could introduce him?

Then I'd met Roger. He'd struck up a conversation with me in the frozen aisle when I was torn between an Arctic Roll and a Viennetta. He advised me to get both.

He was a bank manager, so he didn't need my money—and I let him know that I didn't have as much as people assumed. And he liked American country and western music, so he wasn't after Dave.

He was simply after me.

There were curries and steaks and trips to the cinema. After a couple months, I was just about ready to introduce him to Sam and Katie. Then we went to St. Ives for the weekend. We walked on the beach until rain drove us into the hotel. Over dinner in the hotel's restaurant, he held my hand and smiled into my eyes.

"These potatoes are delicious," I said. "But I'd best stop now."

"Why would you do that?"

"I'm trying to shift some weight. I'll start exercising, too, come Monday."

His green eyes widened in alarm. "Mandy, you can't do that."

"Just try to stop me. I've given up smoking, remember. It's all willpower."

"I mean, don't." He paused. "It's just that—I like you the way you are."

I smiled. "You're sweet. I'm not going to turn into Twiggy, just take off a few stone."

"But I like fat women!" he spluttered.

That had happened two years earlier. In that time, I hadn't had even a casual date. I'd been unlucky three times, and it seemed best to concentrate on work and the kids. And when I decided to open my own salon, it was easier to put romance on the shelf. At the back of the cupboard, really.

But Jack was unlike anyone I'd ever met. Quiet and yet more self-assured than even Dave had been when I first met him. Here was someone I wouldn't mind getting to know. Someone grown-up.

And as the week wore on, I realized I owed Dave an apology. There was no reason, after all, why my children's father shouldn't book an appointment with me. That said, it was a pretty strange way of getting my attention. He could have just called and asked me for a drink.

So, on Friday evening, I watched for Dave from the bay window in the front room, absently petting Butler, my white and grey cat. He arched his back to meet my hand so that I could keep stroking his silky fur with one finger.

When Dave's black Volkswagen Golf pulled up, I turned to the kids, who stood beside me, satchels in hand.

"Wait here a moment. I need to talk to your dad."

Then I walked out to meet him.

He rolled down the window. "Hello, Mandy."

"Robbie did a good job," I said. He had, too. Without removing much hair, he'd made Dave's cut more modern and streamlined.

"He did. In fact, I'll recommend him to anyone looking for a good haircut. Very nice bloke. Easy to talk to."

"Unlike his boss. Dave, I'm sorry for having a go at you in front of him."

Amusement lurked in his light blue eyes. "I expect I deserved it, turning up at your place like a bad penny."

"You had a distinctly guilty look, hiding behind that newspaper." I giggled. "You know, when we saw David Davies in the diary, we were sure you were a fat little Welshman."

"I'm half Welsh, so you're half right."

"Anyway, I'm sorry about that outburst."

"No worries. But, Mandy, I mean it. About wanting to talk. I thought maybe we could have dinner tomorrow, the four of us, and then talk. You and me."

The November evening was colder than I'd expected, and I'd ventured outdoors without a coat. I wrapped my arms around myself.

"And then talk," I repeated.

He gulped. "And then talk."

Was he suggesting a date? Of course, he might just want to talk about maintenance. Perhaps he was low on funds.

"I can't," I said. "I'm having dinner with a friend tomorrow night."

"The same friend you had a drink with Tuesday?"

"Yes."

He smiled wryly. "Well, maybe some other time, then."

There was a pause. "I'll get the kids," I said hurriedly. "See you later."

Inside, Sam and Katie were peering out the window. At least they hadn't heard any of the exchange.

"Well, your dad's here," I said brightly. Of course, he was. "Off you go."

As we walked through the front door, Katie turned to me. Her double blonde ponytails framed her face with its slightly upturned nose and large blue eyes.

"Why were you talking to Daddy just now, Mummy?" she asked.

"Maybe they had business to discuss," said Sam. He was adorably self-important. Tall for ten, he had Dave's lanky, athletic build and brown hair though his eyes were dark like mine.

"But Mummy never talks to Daddy at the car. She waves from the door, and they talk on the telephone." She faced me on the front step, arms folded, her blue eyes watching me carefully.

There was no putting anything over on that one.

"Well, there's a time for everything," I said lightly.

And maybe even a time for romance, I thought, as I waved and the Golf disappeared into the night.

Four

Saturday was manic as it always was. Most of the clients were regulars although there were a couple new punters. I didn't think the *Evening Standard* brought them there, though: when they looked in the mirror, they were interested in their hair and not me.

At half five, I was in the loo, trying to get the ammonia from Sally Stearns' permanent off my hands. A fist rapped at the door.

"Just a moment," I called.

"A bloke's here to see you," Emmy said in a stage whisper. "His name is Jack."

Perhaps he was the early bird after the worm.

"Tell him I'll be a few minutes," I called.

First, I changed my pink boiler suit for a belted red dress with black polka dots. Then I exchanged my flats for heels. A bit of hair gel, a tad more mascara, and some red lipstick, and I was presentable again.

Jack was sitting in the waiting area, a *Financial Times* in hand. We exchanged smiles, and I lifted a finger to let him know I would be a moment longer.

Rose was wrapping up with a client, but Robbie and Emmy were clustered around the desk.

"I'm leaving a little early tonight," I began.

Robbie lifted one arched eyebrow.

"We can see that," said Emmy.

She always had something to say, that one.

"Are you all right to close, Robbie?" I asked.

"Oh, we'll be fine," he said airily.

"Thanks, love. Good night, Emmy, good night, Rose," I called. I waved and walked quickly to the waiting area before Emmy could say anything else.

Jack rose at my approach. "Good evening, Mandy. You look beautiful."

It had been a long time since anyone had said that. "Thank you."

He was looking quite distinguished himself with his dark grey suit and keen blue eyes. My tummy gave a little turn, something it hadn't done in years.

"Shall we go?"

He offered me his arm, and I took it. As we stepped out the door and into the evening, I caught a whiff of his aftershave. It suited him: masculine, but understated with subtle spices and musks.

"I realize I never asked you what sort of food you like," said Jack. "Do you like Italian food?"

"I love it."

"Excellent. I've got reservations at San Lorenzo in Knightsbridge. Good food and discreet service."

He'd managed to get a reservation at San Lorenzo. Ever since it had become known as one of Princess Diana's favorite restaurants, it had become close to impossible to get a table there.

His car was parked just down the street from Luxor. It was a silver two-door Mercedes SL. It reminded me of him for some reason—assured, but not showy.

I laughed as he held the passenger door for me. "Weren't you taking a risk making a reservation? For all you knew, I might hate Italian food."

"I took an educated risk, like I do in my work. There was a good chance I'd be right, and I was."

"But what if I'd said I'd hated it?"

It was his turn to laugh. "I'll not get off lightly with you, Mandy. Then I would have canceled my reservation, and we would have gone elsewhere."

"You would have gotten a table at a decent restaurant? Without reservations on a Saturday night?"

"There are a few places where I can always get a table."

He spoke so quietly and confidently that I knew it must be true. He wasn't bragging, just stating a fact.

We'd arrived at San Lorenzo. I'd often walked or driven past it, but I'd never eaten there. I held my head a little higher as we stepped under the white awning and into the foyer.

Inside the smell of garlic greeted us. The maître d', a middle-aged man with olive skin, bowed and beamed.

"Ah, Mr. Slayton, it is so nice to see you again. You are at the usual table."

We followed him through a dimly lit room, past candlelit tables, where couples chatted quietly. He led us into a conservatory to a table for two behind a small palm tree.

As the maître d' held my chair, I wondered how frequently Jack patronized San Lorenzo and how many women he took there.

"Would you like to start with some wine, Mr. Slayton?" asked the maître d'.

"Will it be red or white, Mandy?" asked Jack.

"Red since it's Italian."

"Some of the 78 Burgundy, Antonello. Grazie."

Over the candles, Jack regarded me. "I come here often on business," he said. "You can speak privately here."

So he'd read my mind.

The maître d' appeared with our wine, we ordered our meals, and then we toasted each other.

"A weekend without the bairns," remarked Jack, a slight smile about his lips.

"Yes, they're with their dad."

His eyes studied me. "Do you worry about them?"

"No, his flat is in Shepherd's Bush, so I could be there in fifteen minutes or so on the A4."

"I meant the lifestyle, I suppose."

I laughed. "Oh, they're quite safe with Dave. He doesn't live much like a rock 'n' roller these days. It's a lot of ice lollies and football in the park."

Brow furrowed slightly, Jack leaned forward. "He pulls his own weight, I trust? Maintenance and such?"

I twirled a lock of hair around my finger. "He pays what he can. He doesn't earn a lot from session work, but he's always on time." Why were we talking about my ex-husband on our first real date?

"Glad to hear it."

"He's always been a good dad; I'll say that much for him."

Why was I defending Dave? I had to change the subject. "Do you have kids?"

"No, my ex-wife and I had no children."

A young waiter brought breadsticks, and we talked of other things.

Jack was a good conversationalist. He told me stories about his work and the people he met.

"I can see why you're a property developer," I said. "It must be exciting, turning nothing into something."

Jack paused, his fork in the air. "Well, you've experienced that first-hand. You've started a business."

"Look, I had an idea, and people happened to like it. And most of my clients followed me to Luxor from my previous salon, so I can't even take credit for luring them with the mummies."

His gaze was intent. "Like I said the other day, you made your own luck, Mandy. No, you'll have to accept being a success."

Our eyes met over my glass. His were so very blue.

"Oh, go on, then," I said.

"I will. I think you've got something special here. No need to stop at one salon."

I put down my glass. "What do you mean?"

"I meant the world needs another Luxor."

I laughed. "I've got my hands full as it is."

"You'd hire someone to run the other salon. But you've got a pow-erful idea, and you've got people following you. That's three-quarters of the battle."

A giggle escaped me as I imagined Robbie, Rose, and Emmy trailing me around London.

Again, Jack seemed to read my mind. "Your customers followed you to Luxor. You made the *Evening Standard*. You've got a reputation now."

"As the ex-wife of a drummer."

"Well, the *Evening Standard* knows people like a gossip. But even if they come out of curiosity, they'll stay because of the atmosphere and the quality of your work. And your regulars have no interest in your past. They know what you can do for them."

I sipped the last of my Burgundy. It was true: my regulars didn't know my ex-husband used to be a successful drummer. Unless they'd read the *Evening Standard* on that fateful day.

"Would you like dessert, Mandy?" Jack asked.

"I'd love to, but no thank you."

He didn't press, thank God. "Well, let's be off, then."

I was aware of his aftershave as he helped me put on my coat. "Can I give you a lift home?"

I shook my head. "Thanks, but I drove today."

"Then I'll drive you to your car."

People teemed by us in groups or pairs, laughing. Occasionally, shouts emerged from open doors. And yet, I felt oddly insulated from it as Jack drove back to Chelsea.

"Here it is."

We stopped in front of my Cavalier. I'd managed to find a spot only a few streets from Luxor that morning.

"Thank you for dinner, it was lovely," I said. All of a sudden, I felt shy, like a teenager on her first date.

"The pleasure was mine. May I see you again?"

He asked for my number, and I wrote it on a slip of paper I dug out of my bag.

Jack lifted my hand to his lips, his stubble grazing my hand. "Good night, Mandy."

From the inside of the car, I watched him retreat around the corner. Had the evening been real?

For the first time since my early twenties, I felt as though I'd entered a fairytale.

Five

When Dave dropped off the kids on Sunday evening, he brought them to the front door. This was a first. Usually, he remained in the Golf while they raced to the house.

I opened the door. Katie and Sam stood on either side of Dave in jeans and jumpers, but my eyes flitted to his face first.

I must have looked surprised, for Dave laughed. "Hello, Mandy. Thought you might like this lot back."

"Mostly." I bent to kiss Katie's cheek and then Sam's. Sam flinched a bit; he didn't relish being embraced in front of others, including his father.

"Did you have a nice time with your dad?" I asked. I was surprised at how natural my voice sounded. All those years in the salon had helped me sound cheerful when I felt anything but.

"Yes," said Sam automatically.

"It was all right," said Katie. Her ponytails bounced as she shifted from one foot to the other. "Can I have ice cream?"

"Not till after your tea and only if you've not had any today."

"I didn't."

"Now say goodbye to your dad, and in you go."

Sam shook hands solemnly with his father, Dave kissed Katie's cheek, and the kids raced up the stairs to their rooms.

Once again, my eyes met Dave's. His blue eyes were laughing.

"She had an ice lolly this afternoon," he said.

"She was counting on you not to rat her out."

"I wouldn't have, but she left me no choice. United front and all."

I expected him to say goodbye and return to the Golf, but he hesitated on the front step. His smile was sheepish as he shifted his weight from one foot to the other just as Katie had a few minutes earlier.

He looked like a child waiting for something.

"Do you want to come in?" I asked.

His blue eyes brightened, and he gave a quick little nod. "Thanks."

That was it.

Dave stepped into the foyer, and I closed the door behind him.

He glanced around the foyer, taking in the small skylight and hanging baskets. "This is nice, Mandy. You always had good taste."

I didn't recall him praising my decorating when we were married. "Thanks."

He stuck his hands in his pockets as though he didn't quite know what to do with them. If I had drumsticks, I would have put them in his hands. Then he wouldn't have looked so bereft.

Suddenly, his lips lifted into a smile beneath his mustache.

"There you are," he said to someone or something behind me. Then he knelt down.

Butler was sauntering toward us. He paused to rub against my leg, but proceeded to Dave.

Dave, still kneeling, patted his head. When he ceased to pet him, the cat tapped his arm with one white paw.

"He remembers you!" I exclaimed.

Of course, Butler greeted everyone who came to the house—that's how he'd earned his name. But his brilliant green eyes were particularly soft, and he purred loudly as Dave stroked him.

"I remember he made a cat person of you."

Dave chuckled. "He's all right."

The ice had been broken.

"I saw Sam shake hands with you just now," I said. "Is that new?"

"It's been going on about six months or so. He started looking embarrassed when I hugged him, but he stood up a bit straighter when I extended my hand my one day."

"He's quite grown up, isn't he? He's protective of Katie and a bit bossy sometimes."

"Very much the big brother." Dave paused. "Mandy, I know you usually give them their tea on Sundays, but—"

"But what?" I asked quickly.

He was studying Butler carefully. "I wondered if you wanted to go to the pub. Just around the corner. They do a nice Sunday roast, and I thought we could go there, the four of us. For tea."

For what seemed like ages, I stood there with my mouth open. Was he asking if we could go out as a family? Meanwhile, he kept on stroking Butler, who gazed at him with blatant adoration.

"I—" I began.

Behind us, in the front room, the phone chimed. I had the notion it was interrupting us on purpose.

I stepped into the front room and returned to the hall with the receiver pressed to my ear.

"Hello?" I said, smiling at Dave. His blue eyes were soft.

"Hi, Mandy," said a Scots voice on the other end.

"Hi, Jack."

Now, Dave's gaze shifted to Butler.

"How are you?"

"Brilliant!" I replied brightly.

"Excellent. Mandy, I want to see you again. How about lunch on Tuesday? Would one o'clock suit? I could do earlier if needs be."

"One o'clock on Tuesday suits."

Butler had moved on. He rubbed once against my legs before loping into the front room, probably to his favorite spot on the settee.

Dave rose to his feet.

"Goodbye, Mandy," he said quietly.

"But—" I began.

"What's that?" asked Jack on the other end of the line.

But Dave had already closed the door and disappeared into the night.

Six

Tuesday dawned sunny and mild for early November. I felt optimistic as I put the kids on the bus and drove to Chelsea. The sun was shining, our diary was full, and I had a lunch date with Jack.

But when I stepped through the salon's doors, Robbie's face was anything but sunny. Beneath his spiky red hair, his green eyes were stormy.

"Good morning—" I began.

"It isn't a good morning, darlin', and it won't be a good day. Emmy's called in again."

I slammed my handbag onto the counter and sank onto the chair behind it. "No."

"I'm afraid so. Though, to do her credit, she left a message on the answering machine last night. She anticipated the splitting headache she would have this morning, and there's a terrible virus sweeping through her house."

"Brought on by too many Blue Lagoons on Saturday night no doubt."

"Undoubtedly, Mandy darlin', but what are you going to do about it?"

"You, Rose, and I will hustle a little more, and I'll buy the three of us a drink after work."

Robbie's eyes sparkled with pleasure, but his voice was serious. "That's what we're doing today, and I won't say no to a drink. But what are you going to do about Emmy?"

He would ask questions like that. "Oh, I'll have a go at her tomorrow." I spoke with more confidence than I felt.

"I imagine that will be as effective as the last chat you had with her."

The cheek! I opened my mouth to retort, but at that moment, Rose entered the salon, clutching both a drawstring bag and a brown paper bag that held her lunch, her tiny green pumps clicking as she approached the desk.

"Good morning, you all right?" she said.

Robbie answered for me. "Everything is not all right. No Emmy again today."

Rose rolled her large dark eyes. Even irate, she looked lovely.

She quickly recovered herself. "I'm happy to take Emmy's clients. If there's no conflict with mine."

"You're in luck, darlin'," said Robbie. "She's just got one appointment at three, and there's no conflict."

She nodded briskly. "Excellent."

"Thanks, love," I said. "We couldn't manage without you."

Her smile transformed her entire face. Funny how happy an honest compliment made people.

It was no wonder that Rose was steadily building a list of clients. The punters loved Emmy's bubbly personality, and Rose could be reserved, even standoffish. But Rose's work was excellent, and clients came away feeling seen and heard.

We got through the next three hours as we had so many other days. Rose greeted clients, answered the phone, and swept the floor when she wasn't seeing clients of her own. That morning, she had a trim and a permanent, so Robbie and I jumped in with the broom and phone when she was occupied.

It went more smoothly than I had expected, which shouldn't have come as a surprise. After all, given Emmy's history, the three of us had it down. But as I trimmed fringes and swept the floor and asked people about their holidays, a tiny, secret part of me looked forward to my lunch with Jack. It was my reward for putting up with Emmy and having to do more than my usual share.

At five of one, just as I was about to show Minty Paige her new do, I heard a Scots voice at the front of the salon.

"I'm here to see Mrs. Wilt," said Jack. He was soft-spoken, but there was a quiet authority in his voice.

"She's just finishing with a client; she'll be with you shortly," replied Robbie airily.

I turned Minty's chair to face the mirror. "Don't you look lovely," I declared with more warmth than necessary. "That shade of blonde really suits you."

Minty smiled a little smugly. Of all my clients, she needed praise the least. At twenty-six, she was already the editor of a top women's monthly. She'd let this and the fact that she could have modeled in the magazine go to her head.

"Thanks," she said coolly. "Shall we schedule for six weeks, then?"

"Of course," I replied. "Robbie will look after you up front."

I led Minty to the desk. As I approached the front of the salon, Jack rose from a chair in the waiting area. His eyes locked with mine, and he smiled.

"Hello, Mandy," he said. "Shall we go?"

"Let me grab my coat."

A minute later, and I was leaving the salon on Jack's arm. As we stepped through the door onto the street, Minty's eyes were on my back. Jack might be twice her age or nearly so, but she recognized him as an attractive—and eligible—man. I couldn't resist shooting her a glance over one shoulder. Her green eyes, usually bored, were wide. She didn't expect to see her stylist on the arm of a distinguished man.

I held my head a little higher as we stepped onto the King's Road.

"I've booked us a table at a little place in Knightsbridge," Jack said once we were in the street. "There's something I'd like to show you. If it's too far, let me know. I don't want to cut into your time with clients."

I shook my head. "It's fine. But what is this thing you want to show me?"

Jack's eyes narrowed to blue slits. "Wouldn't you like to know?"

It was only our second or third date, depending on whether you counted the initial drink, and he was already surprising me. But what was this thing he had to show me? I knew there were a lot of new restaurants and offices being built there; perhaps he wanted to show me a piece of property he was developing.

That could only mean one thing: Jack wanted to share something with me or impress me. When blokes do that, you know they're really interested.

The restaurant proved to be a small café not far from Harrods. We had smoked salmon sandwiches with chardonnay.

"How's business been?" asked Jack.

"Steady, sometimes hectic. Especially today."

"What's different about today?"

"Well, the thing is, it isn't really that different."

Once again, I found myself describing Emmy's habit of calling in and our methods of coping with it. "But we make it work, Robbie and Rose and me."

Eyes hard, Jack listened to me intently.

"What are you going to do about it?" he asked when I finished.

"Have a little chat with her, I suppose."

"Have you chatted before?"

I sighed. "That's the thing. I've let her know that I don't like it and that her clients will be put off if she doesn't show up. And she's already lost clients because of it: some of them have started asking for Rose instead of her."

"And that's not put a stop to it?"

"N-no." Somehow, explaining it all to Jack made me feel silly, like a teacher who couldn't control her students.

"She's no good for the business." Jack took a bite of his sandwich as though the matter were settled.

"Yes, she is," I declared. "Emmy's got a lovely personality—clients love her—and she's got a real feel for hair."

"And if she's not showing up, she can't charm the punters or do their hair," said Jack quietly.

I sighed. "You're right. But she's young, she's had a hard life, and she really wants to be a hairdresser."

"All of us were young once, many people have had hard lives, and most of us still made it to work. If she really wants to make a go of being a hairdresser, she'd be at Luxor five days a week even if she had to work through a hangover now and then. She's hurting her own chances, and if she keeps at it, she'll bring down the salon."

Jack paused.

"You're a soft touch, Mandy," he said finally, "and that's to be admired in a woman. I know you want to be kind to this girl, but think about your own children. What will become of them if your salon closes?"

I studied my sandwich. Whoever prepared it had removed the crusts and added just enough greens to add flavor and texture without overwhelming the salmon. There was an art to making sandwiches just like styling hair.

Jack had the tact to change the subject. We talked about sport. Jack supported the Rangers Football Club, but his passion was rugby. Somehow, I wasn't surprised.

After we finished our sandwiches, Jack took my hand. "Shall we go?" he asked with a smile.

He led me down the street, occasionally casting little glances in my direction. There was something almost boyish about his excitement.

"Do you want me to close my eyes?" I asked.

"That won't be necessary. Here we are."

We stopped in front of a three-story brick Victorian building. The ground floor was an empty shop. A To Let sign hung in the window.

This was what he had been so excited to show me? "It's an empty shop," I said dully.

Jack's eyes shone. "Or the future home of Luxor II."

Stepping closer, I peered into the window. The walls were plain brick, but the ceilings were high and the room spacious.

"You can't deny it's got possibilities," he continued.

"If you installed some mirrors and sinks . . ."

Smiling, Jack nodded.

"And I could commission some more murals with pharaohs and mummies," I added.

"I knew you'd see it, Mandy," he said.

"And it's a growing neighborhood—" I began with more energy.

"With offices full of young professionals who'd welcome a trendy salon."

"I'll think about it," I said.

But what I was really thinking about was that Jack believed in Luxor. In my ability to manage two salons even though I couldn't manage one girl who was always calling in.

He believed in me.

"Think and act. This one will go quickly."

"You're very eager to have me rent this place. Are you sure you're not an estate agent?" I asked, smiling up at him.

"I'm a property developer, not a bloody estate agent. I see potential and act on it. I don't exaggerate it."

Jack pulled me to him. Beneath his grey jacket, his arms were strong, and there was the scent of his aftershave. Swiftly, he kissed me on the mouth.

If we hadn't been on a busy street in broad daylight, I don't know how long our embrace would have lasted.

Seven

After that, Jack and I saw each other two, sometimes three, times each week depending on his schedule. We had dinner at San Lorenzo and little places with quiet waiters and menus that didn't list prices. Sometimes, we caught lunch, usually in a pub or a café near Luxor. Often, he'd show me a vacant storefront or another space that he thought would be ideal for the next Luxor. The spot in Knightsbridge had been snapped up just as Jack said it would.

"Best not dally on this one, Mandy," he'd say. "This part of London's up and coming; it'll go quickly."

It was sweet, really, this interest in my business.

"You're really keen for me to open another salon," I'd reply.

"I'm keen to see Luxor grow. And there's the little matter of the proprietress."

His eyes would meet mine, and for the moment, even if we were in the middle of a busy street with people teeming all around us, we would be all alone.

And he'd ring me every day. We'd have proper conversations—not the perfunctory calls other blokes made. He'd tell me about his work, and he wanted to hear every detail of my work and my life with the kids. He chuckled at what Katie and Sam had said. He was concerned about Emmy's continued absences.

"She'll bring down the business, Mandy," he'd declare. "I know you mean to be kind, but think of Robbie and Rose and their chances."

"You're right," I'd say quickly and change the subject.

I'd never talked as easily with any man as I did with Jack, except maybe Dave when we were going out and when we were first married. And while we'd never been at a loss for words or short of laughs, Dave had never been all that interested in my work. Oh, he'd listen to me rant about a customer or Nettie, the girl I couldn't stand at my first job, but he never acted as though hairdressing were a career. It was how we'd met and something girls did until they found a bloke to look after them.

One evening, when Jack and I had been seeing each other for about a month, he surprised me over dinner.

We were at San Lorenzo. We had finished our pasta and were lingering over our wine. Candlelight cast a soft glow over the table. As I sipped my Chianti, Jack leaned back, one arm over the back of his chair while the other hand held his glass carelessly. A slight smile flitted over his mouth, and his blue eyes were bright.

"So I think you've given up on London, Mandy," he said lazily.

This didn't sound like Jack at all.

"I most definitely have not," I declared. "I've always been a Londoner and always will be."

"Just like I'll always be a Glasgow lad, no matter where life takes me. But I meant business, Mandy."

His eyes were playful. Was he mocking me?

"If you think I've given up on Luxor just because of Emmy—"

"I wasn't talking about her or the salon itself. I meant Luxor II."

I stared at him. "What do you mean?" Did he think I was unambitious just because I hadn't rented any of the spaces he'd shown me?

"I keep showing you promising locations, and you turn up your nose at them. Or you dally until someone else snaps them up."

"I'm not sure that's giving up on London—"

"But what if Luxor II opened in another city? Let's say . . . Liverpool."

Something fluttered in my belly. "Why Liverpool?"

"It's up and coming. I'm looking at a couple properties there. I thought we could drive up the weekend before Christmas and see how Luxor might fare in Liverpool."

He was asking me to go away for the weekend. We'd not been to bed yet though it had been in the air for a couple weeks.

I must have been silent for a minute longer than necessary for he asked, "Well, what do you think, Mandy?"

"Yes, please," I said. My voice was shy, not like itself at all.

Jack reached across the table and took my hand. His eyes were softer than usual as his fingers pressed mine, and once again, I felt that eager little flutter in my belly.

I hadn't been that excited about being with a man since I met Dave in my early twenties.

There were some arrangements to make before we could go away. Robbie agreed to look after Butler and the house, and Dave was happy to mind the kids though it wasn't his usual weekend with them.

Dave picked up the kids that Friday morning. They were still upstairs getting ready when he arrived.

I heard his knock and opened the door. Smiling almost shyly, he stood on the threshold, his hands stuck deep in his coat pockets.

"Hello, Mandy," he said.

"They're still getting ready. It's cold; you'd better come in."

"Thanks." There was real gratitude in his voice as he stepped over the threshold.

He stood uncertainly in the foyer as he had that time last month. Since then, we'd chatted a bit whenever he picked up or returned the kids.

As he'd entered the house, he'd removed his hands from his coat pockets. Now, he thrust them in his pockets again as though the hall were too cold for them.

"So Liverpool, then."

"Yes. Jack's developing some properties, and he wants to show me one."

Dave's eyes swiftly became hooded. "Are you buying properties together?"

For some reason, I felt self-conscious, and to hide it, I laughed.

"Hardly. It's not as though I'd bring much capital to any investment, would I?"

Dave looked down. He'd taken my remark as a jibe about the financial state he'd left me in.

To spare his feelings, I said hurriedly, "It's just that Jack thinks Luxor has a lot of potential. He says I could expand, open another salon. He's shown me a couple sites in London, and now he wants me to look at a place in Liverpool."

Dave's eyes rose, and his mouth formed a crooked smile.

"Is that what you want, Mandy?" he asked quietly. "To be a businesswoman with a chain of salons?"

I opened my mouth, then shut it. "Is that such a bad thing? Doesn't Mrs. Thatcher say that we're a nation of shopkeepers?"

Dave scowled. "What about the poor fuckers who can't find a shop or mine or factory to work in? Or a studio for that matter?"

He hadn't had much luck finding work as a session musician, I knew. I would have to steer the conversation to less personal channels.

"Jack says Mrs. Thatcher is turning the country around," I said. "We'll all reap the benefits eventually."

Now, Dave grimaced. "Oh, God, Maggie. She's like some awful headmistress with that grating voice and helmet hair."

Truth be told, I couldn't stand her voice either. I had to change the television channel or radio station whenever the prime minister spoke. But I was bound to defend her.

"Isn't that a very . . . sexist remark?"

Under his mustache, Dave's upper lip curled slightly. "What, are you women's lib now, too?"

I wasn't sure if I was. "What if I am? Anyway, Mrs. Thatcher wants people to work hard and save their money. What's wrong with that?"

"Nothing—if they've got a job to get to."

Put that way, I agreed with him, but I couldn't let him see that.

I tossed my hair. "Anyhow, you complained enough about the other lot when they were in power."

"Well, the taxes were a bit much in the seventies." Dave ran a hand through his hair. "Hard to save anything under Labor."

"I suppose the fact that you owned five cars at once had nothing to do with it," I snapped.

Dave's eyes met mine, we laughed, and he extended his hand. The truth was neither of us had ever been much for politics.

"Touché, Mandy. Let's call a truce, shall we?"

Before I could take his hand, something brushed against my calf. It was Butler. He arched his white and grey back to meet my hand before repeating the performance with Dave.

Dave knelt to pet the cat. As soon as he ceased to pat him, Butler tapped his arm with one immaculate white paw.

"You named him well, Mandy," said Dave. "Good job his manners are better than ours."

Just then the kids came racing down the stairs, dragging their bags behind them.

"Daddy!" Katie cried, rushing into his arms.

"Hi, Dad," said Sam. His tone was mild, but I could see the pleasure in his face.

"Hello, sweetheart," said Dave, hugging Katie. Then he extended a hand to Sam. "Hi, mate."

In his way, he was sensitive, knowing how to greet each child. And both of them were delighted to see him.

Then Katie turned to me.

"What were you and Daddy rowing about?" she asked.

"Katie, shush!" said Sam, shooting a glance at his sister.

"Politics," Dave replied. "Don't ever get started on it. Now you'd best say goodbye to your mum."

Both of the kids hugged me in turn. Sam embraced me quickly as though I might carry a disease, but Katie returned my kiss on the cheek.

"Be good in Liverpool, Mummy," she said. "Will you fight about politics with your friend?"

The cheeky monkey! I was about to reprove her when I caught Dave's eye over her blonde ponytails.

"Well, off with you, then." I kissed them both one more time.

"Goodbye, Mandy," said Dave. Tiny lines formed around his eyes.

From the bay window in the front room, I watched the trio walk to Dave's car. Butler sat in the window seat, and I stroked his silky fur absently.

Katie held one of Dave's hands while he carried her bag with the other. On the other side of his father, Sam strode, turning to him and smiling occasionally as they approached the Golf.

They were really excited, bless them, about what the weekend had in store. And they were simple pleasures, all of them, a walk in the park, Cadbury Dairy Milks, perhaps the cinema.

For a moment, I envied them.

Eight

That afternoon, we took the M1 to Liverpool. Jack's Mercedes overtook other cars without seeming to speed outright. It was quiet and confident like Jack himself. Then I remembered that I was thirty-four, too old to compare men to their cars.

"Christmas is coming, Mandy," said Jack as he overtook a Peugeot. "Will you see family?"

I sighed. "Probably. It's what you do, isn't it."

He shot me a laser glance. "You make it sound like a punishment."

I laughed. "It's not as bad as all that. My mum and her husband, Mark, own a little bed and breakfast in Torquay, but they generally spend a few days up country between Christmas and the New Year. Mum does her duty with Kate and me and our families, and then she races back to the West Country."

"Do they stay with you?"

"When I was married to Dave and we had a bigger house, they did. These days, she stays with Kate and Jon in Middlesex."

The steely blue eyes flicked a glance at me. "You're not close."

I laughed again, a bit sheepishly this time. "To be honest, no. Mum did her best with us, but she liked being a wife and girlfriend better than being a mum. Our dad took off when Kate was a baby, and she had to fend for herself and us. When we grew up and left home, I expect it was a bit of a relief to her." I didn't want Jack to feel sorry for me or think I wanted his pity, so I laughed again. "Can't blame her, really. We were little nightmares."

In the mirror, Jack's eyes were softer than usual, even concerned. "And your sister? You've not mentioned her much."

"Kate? We get on all right. She's three years younger, so I looked after her a bit when we were kids."

"And then?"

"When I met Dave, I was able to do a bit more for her. We paid her fees at a smart secretarial college, so that gave her a start."

"But no gratitude?"

Again, I laughed. "Oh, Kate's grateful. She always has been. But she doesn't need me."

"You named your daughter after her." It was a statement, not a question.

"You're very keen, you know. They're both called Katherine, so I suppose I did. But Katie is still very much a Katie, and I'm not sure Kate was even as a little girl."

The corners of Jack's eyes wrinkled. Then he became serious.

"So when you became a hairdresser and opened Luxor, you did it all on your own. With no support at all."

I frowned. "I wouldn't say that. Mum was glad when I did a hair-dressing course and later when I opened the salon. And it was because of Dave that I was able to open Luxor. The divorce settlement and everything."

Now it was Jack's turn to frown. "But did anyone ever tell you had talent? Good job and such?"

"No." Dave had thanked me and complimented my work the day we'd met and I'd cut his hair, but I knew that wasn't what Jack meant.

"And that's what makes you remarkable," Jack declared. "You've done it all on your own without money or advice from anyone."

I giggled. "Well, my instructor, Miss Moffat, once told me I'd done a good bubble. But she set me straight on beehives."

"I'll have none of that, Mandy. You made your own luck."

He lifted my hand to his lips. His mouth grazed my fingers and the inside of my wrist.

"What about you?" I asked.

"I'm lucky now," he murmured as he kissed the inside of my wrist one more time.

So was I.

"Did you get any encouragement at home?" I persisted.

For a moment, Jack remained silent, his eyes on the road.

"Not really," he said finally. "And that's no complaint against my mum or dad. There were five of us all very much of an age, and both of them worked. Dad was a builder, and Mum took in laundry. So there wasn't much attention for any of us, and as I was smack in the middle, there was a bit less for me."

Jack had never mentioned his family, and somehow, I hadn't felt right asking him about them. So I was honored he was confiding in me.

"Do you see much of them?"

"My dad's been gone fifteen years and my mum eight." Once again, his eyes were straight on the road ahead.

"I'm sorry."

"I'm on good terms with my three sisters and my brother. I'll say this much for them: none of them have ever asked me for anything."

It was my turn to shoot a sidelong glance at Jack. "But you'd help them if they needed it."

Jack's brow furrowed. "'Needs' a funny word, a funny word indeed. Would I make sure they had a roof over their heads and food to eat? Aye, of course. Do I remember 'em at Christmas and on their birthdays? Yes. But there are certain things a man and woman have got to work for."

I remembered when Dave and I first got together. Serval was just about at its peak, and shops that had been beyond my reach were suddenly within it. Dave bought me anything I wanted or that he thought I wanted, and he bought clothes and cars for himself as well. And he'd been so eager to help people or, at least, to buy them things. On the spur of the moment, he'd surprise old friends with color televisions or show up to stand a round of drinks. And he couldn't do enough for his parents or sister or for my family either. It was he who'd suggested paying for Kate's education.

"But your nieces and nephews? You'd help them?"

Jack's mouth tightened. "If they show initiative, they can count me as a friend."

So someone had sought his assistance and been found wanting.

"Can I ask what happened?"

Jack's voice was warm. "You can ask anything you like, Mandy. It was my sister Susan's son, Allan. He'd a notion to become an estate agent. He'd done well on his exams, so I was happy to get him a place at a friend's firm."

The memory must have stung, for Jack's lips were once again set in a hard line.

I probed gently. "And what happened?"

"At first, nothing much. They were on a way to being pleased with him as he had a good way with the clients and learned quickly. But then he started coming in late and then calling in. Once, he didn't show up when he was supposed to show people a property, and they had to let him go."

"And then?" My voice was higher than usual.

"He talked himself into another role, and the same thing happened."

"Did you ever learn why he was doing this—coming in late and calling in?" I couldn't help but think of Emmy and her habits.

"He drank too much." Jack was crisp and decisive.

"Did anyone help him?" Once again, my voice was oddly shrill and nervous.

Jack's eyes flickered to mine in the mirror. They were steely now.

"Drinking is a choice, Mandy. So is working harder than the next man. Allan chose to drink, and that's why he is where he is today."

I didn't ask where Allan had ended up though I was dying to know.

"Don't get me wrong; Allan's my nephew, and I'll send him something at Christmas. But I can't sacrifice my money and reputation on someone who's not worth it.

"And I don't see the point of handouts," Jack continued. "If my friends or relations want a particular type of television or car, they can bloody well work for it. No, I don't toss pearls before swine."

I couldn't resist. "How about diamonds for dogs?"

His eyebrows contracted. "What's that?"

"A Bowie song. 'Diamond Dogs.'"

"I don't know it."

Of course, he wouldn't. But perhaps he was right. What had Dave accomplished when he sent old mates color televisions or top-notch stereos? Was he just buying their friendship?

Jack must have sensed it was time to change the subject, for when he spoke again it was in a lighter tone.

"In any case, Mandy, I hope you like the spot I've in mind for you. It's near the docks. It's not much now, but in a year or two, it'll be the place to be. And Luxor will be there."

"Ahead of the game."

"That's the idea."

We arrived in Liverpool at around six. Jack had booked a room at the Atlantic Tower Hotel. I'd stayed at some nice hotels when I was married to Dave, but the Atlantic Tower Hotel was impressive with its twelve stories of glowing windows.

Since Jack had reserved a table at the hotel's restaurant, we dined there. Made to look like a restaurant car on a train, it was elegant.

Over roast chicken and champagne, we laughed a great deal. When the waiter brought the dessert cart, Jack insisted I select one.

"You're a terrible influence, you know," I said after my first bite of tiramisu. "I exert willpower when I'm not with you. It's been months since I had a biscuit."

Jack's eyes shone as he pressed my hand. "You deny yourself the mediocre and save up for the best," he said quietly. "That's real pleasure."

I had to admit that the tiramisu was the very best I'd ever tasted.

After we finished our coffee, Jack again reached for my hand across the table.

"Shall we go, Mandy?" His voice was softer than usual.

"Yes, please."

With one arm around my waist, he led me up the stairs. As we walked, we stole little glances at each other. His eyes were warm and faintly conspiratorial.

In our room, we sat down beside each other on the bed. Smiling into my eyes, Jack drew me toward him.

Then his arms were around my shoulders and his mouth was on mine.

"What will you do if I don't take the place by the docks?" I asked when we parted.

Jack was covering my neck and ear with small kisses. His voice was husky when he answered my question.

"Then we'll go to Brighton and Bristol and Leeds and Oxford and Harrogate—"

His hand reached up to turn off the light.

Nine

I decided not to go with the site near the docks. Though Jack had chosen well, I had to admit: it was in an old brick building, it had high ceilings and large windows, and the light, in the late afternoon, would be brilliant.

After the estate agent left, we stood on the pavement, surveying the building.

"It's lovely," I said. "But somehow I can't see myself in Liverpool."

Jack put an arm around my shoulder and kissed my temple.

"Sometimes, you've got to go with your gut, Mandy. I've turned down many a good prospect because of a hunch, and most of 'em have been right. We'll keep looking; we'll find the right spot eventually."

There was something warming about Jack's confidence. He really believed I was capable of running two salons. And he had said "we." That meant he planned to be around for a while.

I nestled my head on his shoulder, and his arm dropped to circle my waist.

As planned, I spent Christmas Day at Kate's house. Since Dave had the kids the next day, Jack and I spent Boxing Day together at his flat on the first floor of a terraced white house in Chester Square.

It was the first time I'd been to his flat, which was sparsely, yet elegantly furnished. After a quiet dinner, we sat on the beige chintz sofa in his lounge in front of a roaring fire, a glass of Burgundy in each of our hands and his arm around my shoulder.

I sent him a sidelong glance over my wine. "You've obviously read the right books and watched the right films."

Jack cocked an eyebrow. "Why?"

"You've assembled all the ingredients for romance. At least, the crackling fireplace and the wine. Are you sure you haven't read Mills & Boon?"

Jack kissed me teasingly, his mouth lingering on mine a few seconds longer than the usual peck.

"I've not had that pleasure, but I'm glad you approve. I have one more item to add to the menu."

Now it was my turn to raise an eyebrow. Was this a new way of seducing me?

Suddenly, Jack was proffering a tiny black box. "Happy Christmas, Mandy."

"Oh!" I exclaimed. My gift for him was still in my bag.

His smile was reassuring. "Open it."

The velvet was soft beneath my fingers as I prized open the box. Inside, on white satin, was a tennis bracelet. Between two strands of gold filigree, tiny diamonds sparkled at me.

"Oh, it's beautiful!" I exclaimed.

"Try it on."

I did. It was elegant and understated, nothing like my usual style. But it was beautiful.

It could become my usual style.

"Thank you, Jack. It's more elegant than anything I've had before."

"Now thank me properly."

His kiss was lingering, probing. When we pulled away, I laughed a little.

"Now I've got something for you. Just a minute."

I rose from the sofa and tiptoed into Jack's room. There, I extracted a small, wrapped parcel from my suitcase. Then I dashed back to the lounge.

"Happy Christmas, Jack," I said as I handed him the gift.

He unwrapped it carefully.

"Open it," I urged, learning forward. I couldn't wait to see his reaction.

He unfolded tissue paper, revealing a tiny ceramic pharaoh with a turquoise and gold headdress.

"I got him at the British Museum gift shop," I said all in a rush. "You've encouraged me so much with Luxor that I wanted to give you something Egyptian. As a token."

It was a child's gift and a child's speech, but Jack's eyes were very bright.

"I've received many gifts over the years, but nothing as thoughtful as that, Mandy. Thank you."

He pulled me toward him and kissed me firmly on the mouth.

"Will you keep him on your desk?" I asked when we parted. "He could urge you to take risks or be stern with employees. Though he doesn't look very intimidating to be honest."

He didn't either. There was something timid about the pharaoh's large, kohl-rimmed eyes and his small mouth.

Jack set his wineglass on the coffee table. "Is that what you think of me? A stern taskmaster?" His voice teased even as his eyes probed.

"Not really. Only compared to me." I studied my wineglass carefully as I wound a finger around its stem.

Jack sighed. "Mandy, it's just that I don't like to see you taken advantage of. This girl Emily—"

"Emmy."

"Emmy may be a very nice girl who's had a rough life. I accept that. But what that has to do with Luxor I cannot say."

I sighed. "Everything you say makes sense. But she's got a real talent for hair, and she's been at Luxor since it opened a year ago—"

"And the salon may not be open another year if she ruins its reputation. And where will that leave Robbie and Rose? And your bairns?"

It was the day after Christmas, I'd just exchanged gifts with the first man I'd loved in years, and we were talking about a junior who called in habitually.

I turned a brilliant smile on Jack. "Speaking of Katie and Sam, it's about time you met them."

"I was thinking the same thing. Perhaps a film. *One Hundred and One Dalmatians* is in the cinema, and then we could all go out for tea."

"Perfect." A cinema outing would be just the thing. There wouldn't be too much pressure to talk, and afterwards we could all chat a bit at the café.

Jack replenished our glasses from the bottle on the coffee table. Then he raised his.

"To us, Mandy. And to Luxor and Katie and Sam. And the New Year. May it hold lots of cause for celebration."

"To us!"

Our glasses clinked, and our eyes met. It had been a long time since I'd had so much to celebrate at Christmas.

***

The next afternoon, Dave returned the kids. They raced into the house, eager to show me their treasures. Katie had a Sindy doll with a rainbow-colored leotard and legwarmers and a few books, including Roald Dahl's *The Witches*, while Sam carried a new football and a Chelsea Football Club shirt. I knew he'd wanted a Miami Dolphins jersey since he and his friends were enthralled with American football, but he seemed pleased with his Chelsea shirt. Like his father, he supported the club.

It was nothing, of course, to what we'd given them when we were married and Serval was at its peak. But I oohed and aahed over the gifts, knowing the real pleasure they brought to the kids and the pleasures Dave had done without to afford them. I guessed he'd sacrificed a few trips to the pub and the chip shop to give them a Christmas.

"Now you bugger off upstairs," said Dave. "I've got to chat with your mum."

Katie's eyes were wide between her two ponytails. "What about, Daddy?" she asked. "Do you have secrets with Mummy?"

Sam shot her a glance. "Shush!"

"That's enough," I said. "Up you both go."

Upstairs they both went with many backward glances on Katie's part. Near the top of the stairs, Sam gave her a small push in the back.

Once the doors of their rooms clicked shut, we looked at each other and laughed.

"A cheeky monkey and a bully boy," I said.

"Siblings," said Dave.

"Speaking of which, did you see Maureen over Christmas?" Maureen was Dave's only sister.

"No, they were with Frank's family this year. But I'll drive up to Wolverhampton tomorrow to spend a couple days with them."

"Lovely." When we were married, Dave hadn't seen much of Maureen though he'd always sent her and her family presents. This was an improvement. "What did you do on Christmas?"

"Not a lot. I played drums in my flat—since my neighbors were shrieking, they weren't in a position to object. Then I went out and got a Chinese. So I was spared the horror of the Christmas film and the crackers."

He smiled as though he didn't want me to feel sorry for him. I did anyway.

"What about you? I heard you had the usual festivities with your mum, Mark, Kate, and Jon. How was it?"

"As ever."

"I don't know whether that's encouraging or discouraging."

I laughed. "A bit of both to be honest. Mark was very pleasant and mildly drunk the whole time, and Mum hurried away whenever anyone spoke to her for more than five minutes at a time. She couldn't wait to get back to Torquay."

"And the Lovely Kate and Jolly Jon?" His voice dripped with sarcasm.

I laughed. "You never cared much for either of them."

"They're all right. And Kate's your sister, so I could tolerate them now and again. Still could if I had to."

And to do Dave justice, he'd always been cordial with them. He'd listened to Jon's stories and admired whatever he'd last purchased. And he'd paid Kate's fees at the secretarial college after all.

Dave stuck his hands in his coat pockets. "Well, the New Year's just around the corner. Any resolutions, Mandy?"

"Funny you should ask. I was just talking about that with someone. I'm going to try to be more decisive at work."

A crooked smile played around the corner of Dave's mouth as he studied the floor. "By someone, I assume you mean Jack."

"Yes." For some reason, I felt oddly defensive, and my tone was more defiant than I intended.

"What about you?" I asked in a softer voice.

"To work more." Dave laughed shortly. "Not much session work these days. The synthesizer should put most of us out of business in the next decade."

"I'm sorry," I said.

"Yes, I know I can't pay much maintenance," said Dave bitterly.

"No, I mean, you're talented, Dave. It's a shame a drummer like you can't get work."

Dave's eyes widened with pleasure. "Thanks, Mandy," he said quietly.

He paused. "So I'm going to look for other work since synths show no sign of going away. Hell, I'll drive a lorry if I have to."

That's how he'd made a living before Serval made it big. "I hope it doesn't come to that, Dave."

He shrugged, averting his eyes. "If it keeps a roof over my head and helps Katie and Sam, it has to be."

Once again, he paused. "And in the New Year, I want to make more time for the people who mean the most to me."

"Katie and Sam?" I couldn't fault him as a father. He took them when it was his turn, and he was always warm and attentive. They were as apt to confide in him as they were in me.

"Yes, and others."

"Maureen and her family?"

"And others."

His light blue eyes studied me carefully. Perhaps this was his way of telling me he had a serious girlfriend.

"Good for them," I said lightly. "Well, thanks for looking after the kids. See you soon."

Dave smoothed his mustache with one hand. Beneath his fingers, another wry smile formed.

"See you next year, Mandy."

He turned on one heel and stepped out the door.

For a moment, I stared at the closed door as though I expected it to open again. I wasn't sure what I was waiting for.

Then again, all our conversations in the foyer had felt odd, unfinished. And something was missing from this one, something that had been there during the other chats.

Butler! That was it. He'd come to greet Dave the other times. Strange that he'd not emerged at the sound of his voice. But he'd not been himself for the past couple days. He'd spent a lot of time sleeping under my bed. I would pick him up, make much of him, and coax him to eat something.

As I went to look for him, it again occurred to me that I had missed something.

Ten

Luxor was closed through the second of January. On the third, Robbie greeted me with a raised eyebrow.

"Happy New Year, Mandy darlin'," he said. "If you expect that the world has changed, you've come to the wrong salon. You'll be astonished to know that Emmy has a headache and an upset stomach."

I tossed my handbag on the desk. "Damn her!" I exclaimed with more vehemence than usual. "She'll bring down the business."

His eyebrow rose higher still. "Undoubtedly, darlin'. And in the meantime, she's making everyone's Thursday a little more miserable."

Poor Robbie. He and Rose had the most to do in Emmy's absence. I put a hand on his sleeve.

"I'm sorry, Robbie. And thanks for everything you do to make Luxor a success. You're an asset to the salon."

His lips smiled, but his eyes doubted. "You make me sound like a chair, darlin'. How was Christmas?"

"It was all right. I saw my mum and my sister. And Jack and I spent Boxing Day together."

"And you exchanged gifts according to the ancient custom."

"Yes. He gave me this." I turned my wrist to show him the bracelet.

"Very nice." His eyes flitted to my face. "But not your usual look."

"Fashions change," I said lightly. "And so do people. How was your Christmas?"

A veil came over Robbie's eyes. "It came and went, darlin'. Damien and Freddie were with their families, so I had a lie-in and got a take-away." He yawned. "It was nice to have the flat to myself for a change."

I could have kicked myself for asking Robbie about Christmas. I should have remembered that he had nowhere to go and that his flatmates would be with their families. Next year, I'd invite him to mine.

Just then, the bell rang, announcing an arrival. Rose entered the salon.

"Happy New—" she began. Our faces must have told the story, for she sighed.

"Oh, no," she said.

"Oh, yes," replied Robbie. "We'll answering more calls and sweeping more hair and cutting more hair and looking after more of Miss Emmy's irate clients."

"I'll do my bit," I said. "You should never expect your staff to do anything you wouldn't do."

"But you always have done," said Rose. Her dark eyes were large and bewildered.

Once again, Robbie's eyebrow hovered near his forehead.

"Are you quite sure Jack didn't give you his brain along with the bracelet?" he asked. "Because you don't sound like yourself."

The cheek! But there wasn't time to reprimand him.

"Let's have a look at the diary," I said. "Then we can see how we can divvy up Emmy's clients if they don't care to reschedule."

Fortunately, Emmy didn't have too many appointments booked that day. That morning, Robbie had a no-show, and I had a cancellation, so we were able to cover Emmy's appointments without stretching ourselves too thin.

That afternoon, Jack took me to lunch at a small café around the corner. His blue eyes surveyed me keenly across the table.

"What's wrong, Mandy?" he asked.

"Is it that obvious?"

"I can tell you're unhappy, and I don't like to see you that way."

I sighed. "It's Emmy. She's called in again. This time, it's a headache and an upset stomach. You've got to give her credit for some kind of honesty."

"You know what I think, Mandy."

"I should sack her."

It was Jack's turn to sigh. "It's for the sake of Luxor. And Robbie and Rose. How many times did she call in in December alone?"

Again, I sighed. "Five."

"That amounts to more than once a week. And the salon was only open for three weeks last month. And how many times did you try to reason with her about it?"

I leaned back in my chair. "About five times over the past year," I muttered.

"Well, then you've given her five chances. More when you consider all the times she's called in and the days she's cost you."

"I didn't pay her for the days she didn't work," I snapped. I paused. "It's just that I dread the conversation, really. It's not something I've ever had to do."

Jack nodded. "The first time's the worst. How about this? After Luxor closes, I'll come round. You'll call the girl then, and I'll be by your side."

I stared at him. He really wanted me to sack this kid.

"We can have a stiffener at the pub beforehand," he said gently.

My face must have shown my dismay. "No drink necessary," I said. "But thanks all the same."

The waitress brought our sandwiches then, and we talked of other things.

After lunch, Jack walked me back to Luxor. He kissed me and pressed my elbow. "See you later, Mandy."

I tried to lift my mouth into a smile, but I made a poor attempt of it.

The afternoon was more chaotic than the morning. I was grateful for the chaos even when Emmy's client was miffed about being kept waiting while Rose finished a permanent and even when one of my regulars, Mrs. Holt, was her most exacting self. It all meant I didn't have to think about what would happen when the salon closed.

But close it did. Shortly after six, Robbie and Rose helped me sweep the last locks of hair from the floor and wipe down the counters.

"Good night, Mandy," said Robbie, flinging his scarf over his neck. "With any luck, we'll be a foursome again tomorrow."

"We'll be all right," I replied. "Good night."

As she stepped out in the street, Rose shot me a glance over her shoulder. She had heard what I didn't say.

I flashed her a brilliant smile even as my stomach lurched.

I envied them as they walked out the door and into the street. Robbie was going to grab a drink and a curry with some mates, Rose was returning to her family in Notting Hill, and neither of them were about to sack someone.

At exactly half-past six, Jack knocked on the salon's door. I held the door for him as though he were an important customer, and then he swept me into his arms for a kiss.

"Hello, Mandy," he said, still holding me. I could smell his after-shave. Kouros by Yves Saint Laurent was his brand as I'd discovered when we'd gone to Liverpool.

I stepped out of his embrace. "Hi, Jack," I said. My voice was flat, unlike itself.

"You're not having misgivings?"

I shook my head. "I'm just not looking forward to it."

"No one does, especially the first time. But I'll be right beside you."

I nodded, and we walked to the desk, Jack's arm around my waist.

"Do you know what you're going to say?" asked Jack.

"Can I run it by you?"

"Of course."

I paused. "Emmy, I've enjoyed working with you, and you're a talented stylist. However, you're not a reliable employee, and for the sake of the salon, I believe it's time we part ways. I will be happy to provide you with an adequate reference."

Jack gave a quick nod. "And if you deliver it with half that convic-tion, you'll have no arguments. And what's more, if there's anything decent about the girl, she'll respect you."

"I hope so."

"Now, Mandy," said Jack gently. "It doesn't matter if a junior likes what you have to say or even if she likes you for that matter. What matters is whether you believe yourself. Because if you don't, the others won't."

He paused. "Do you believe it, Mandy?"

I remembered the days Robbie, Rose, and I had run ourselves ragged covering the salon. I recalled the clients who became irate when Emmy did not appear for their appointments. Finally, Jack's words echoed in my ear: "For the sake of Luxor. And Robbie and Rose."

"Yes," I declared with more conviction than ever before.

Jack smiled. "Excellent. Now dial the number."

I rang Emmy's flat, averting my eyes from Jack.

"Hello?" inquired a shrill female voice I didn't recognize.

"Is Emmy available?"

"Hang on. Emmy! Phone!"

In an instant, Emmy was on the line. "Hello?"

Her voice was young and small. My eyes flitted to Jack for support. He nodded.

"Hello, Emmy, this is Mandy from Luxor," I said. As though she knew a score of Mandys.

"Hiya, you all right?" Now her voice was high, nervous. I'd never called her after hours before.

"Yes." It seemed natural to ask her how she was feeling, but I knew Jack wouldn't approve. Counterproductive, he would call it.

I hesitated. On the other end, the only sound was a television in another room.

"Emmy, I've enjoyed working with you," I began.

There was a slight intake of breath. I opened my mouth, and again Jack gave a little nod.

"You're a talented stylist," I continued. My voice was strange and cold as though I were an actress in a film. "But you're not a reliable employee, and I believe it's time we part ways. Should you seek other employment, I will be happy to provide you with an adequate reference."

Should you seek other employment. As though she had a bloody choice.

"What?" cried Emmy.

"You can collect your things in the morning," I said coolly. "Good night."

I hung up because that was easier than talking.

"Well done," said Jack quietly. "Anyone would think you'd been doing that all your life."

I tried to smile. Clearly, he considered it a compliment.

"How about a drink, then?"

I shook my head. "Thanks, but I've got to go home and collect the kids."

"All right, but you're having dinner with me on Friday."

That evening, Butler refused his wet food and ate only a bit of his biscuits. He'd been eating less of late. His lack of appetite and his new habit of spending hours under my bed worried me.

If anyone knew how to make cats eat, it would be my friend Elsie. She and her husband, Alec, Dave's former bandmate, had two cats of their own, and she was always fostering cats for her local chapter of Cats Protection. It had become her mission along with writing a column for *Hearth and Home*.

So I rang Elsie.

"Mandy! How are you?" she exclaimed. Even after twelve years in Britain, she still sounded like she came from New York, or Jersey City as she always reminded me.

"I'm all right, love. It's Butler I'm concerned about." I explained his lack of interest in food and the time he spent under my bed.

Elsie listened carefully. "There are a couple ways to coax cats to eat," she said finally. "You can handfeed him some of his wet food. Cats love to eat out of their people's hands, and since Butler loves you, he'd probably like it."

She paused. "Or—this sounds silly—you can kiss him on top of his head while offering him food. It mimics what mother cats do—lick their kittens' foreheads whilst they eat. I know it sounds ridiculous." She laughed a bit self-consciously.

"It doesn't sound silly at all. It's worth trying."

She asked about work and the kids, and I asked her about Alec and her writing.

"Oh, my book launch is scheduled for the seventh of February," Elsie said. "It's at Primrose Hill Books in Regent's Park. It would be lovely if you could come. Alec's booked a room at Odette's afterward for supper."

"Of course, I'll be there," I said warmly. "I love your book, and I want to be the first to buy it. I'll want a signed copy, naturally."

"Oh, thanks." There was relief in Elsie's voice. We'd been friends for twelve years, and she was still surprised that I liked her and wanted to attend her do. It was that quality that made me want to take care of her.

"I'm looking forward to it." I paused. "Can I bring someone?"

"A man, you mean?"

"Yes." I felt sheepish, a young girl with her first boyfriend.

"Yes, we'd love to meet him." She sounded really excited. No matter what was going on in her life, good or bad, she had room for others.

We chatted for a couple a more minutes, but before we rang off, Elsie returned to Butler.

"I should take him to the vet, Mandy," she said quietly. "As soon as you can."

"You're right, love," I replied. "I'll schedule an appointment tomorrow."

I replaced the receiver. Of course, she was right. If I were being honest, I'd known it for some time.

With a wry smile, I picked up Butler's dish and walked to my bedroom.

"Hello, Butler," I said.

At the sound of my voice, he emerged from under the bed and rubbed against my outstretched finger. He'd lost weight, but his white fur was as silky as ever.

I placed the dish before him and kissed the top of his head.

Butler bent his little head over the dish and began lapping at the strips of meat and gravy.

It obviously worked. So I kept kissing the top of his head. There was a soft constant clicking as his tiny tongue lapped up the meat and gravy. The sound of Butler eating was the most beautiful thing I'd heard all day. There, in the quiet room, I felt like myself again.

Suddenly, tears streamed down my face.

Eleven

The next morning, I donned my red jumpsuit, the one that always made me feel more confident, and spritzed myself with Coco Chanel. When I stepped into Luxor, I wore a smile.

"It's important to be cheerful if you've had to sack someone," Jack said. "You want your staff to be positive about what's ahead."

Behind the desk, Robbie stood, elbows on the counter, his head resting on his fists.

"Good morning, Robbie!" I called as I entered the salon. My voice was loud, unlike itself.

One delicately arched eyebrow approached his fringe. He looked like an annoyed cat. "Good morning, Mandy."

"How was curry?" I asked, setting my bag on the desk.

"All right, darlin', except for the broken chapati. The waiter dropped it, apologized, and then brought it out of the kitchen again."

I grimaced. "Awful."

"Ted ate it, bless him. He worries me, that boy."

I ran my eyes over the diary. "Does Emmy have any appointments booked today?"

"Just two."

My eyes scanned the page. One before lunch and one before closing. We would be able to cover them.

I nodded. "That should work."

Robbie glanced swiftly at me. "You mean if she calls in again."

"She won't," I said quietly. I kept my eyes on the page.

"Did you have a little chat with her?"

I could have slapped him.

"Yes," I replied in the same quiet voice. "She won't be coming back."

Out of the corner of my eye, I shot Robbie a glance. His green eyes were large, and his face, always fair, was paler than ever.

"You gave her the sack?"

I sighed. "I rang her and let her know it would be best if she pursued other ventures."

There was silence.

"I suggested she seek other employment," I said.

"Oh, I heard you the first time," replied Robbie. He paused. "Changing the words doesn't change the meaning, you know."

I reeled to face him. "I did it for you and Rose," I snapped. "She would have brought down the whole salon and all of us with it."

The doorbell jangled, and Rose entered.

"Hello, Rose, you all right?" I inquired brightly.

"I'm all right, thanks." Her brown eyes were watchful.

She knew. Emmy must have called her after we'd rung off.

There was no use making speeches or explaining my motives. It would only make it worse.

Again, I sighed. "We're a staff of three now. Emmy had two clients scheduled today, a permanent just before lunch and a trim before closing. Rose, could you take on the perm? Robbie, perhaps you could trim Helen Smith's hair after Mrs. Garnett's dye?"

They nodded, and their eyes did not meet mine.

Like all the days without Emmy, the morning was a blur. Rose was getting more and more of her own clients, so Robbie and I did our share of making tea, answering the phone, and sweeping up hair. But unlike the other days, there was no easy banter between us. Rose was withdrawn and Robbie tense. When our eyes met, he smiled tightly.

Later in the morning, I called the vet's surgery.

"I'm afraid we don't have any openings until next week," said the receptionist. "Could you come next Tuesday at eleven?"

"But Butler's not eating!" I exclaimed.

Immediately, she became more sympathetic. "If he's not eating or drinking, we can see him today. We have an opening at three."

Part of me wanted to leap at it. I would call my clients, apologize profusely, and reschedule. But I couldn't lie.

"He is eating and drinking, just not as much as usual. And he's a bit lethargic. I'll take the appointment next Tuesday."

"Are you sure?"

"Yes."

Slowly, I replaced the receiver. Was I letting down Butler just as I had Rose and Robbie?

Jack and I had lunch at a pub across the road. Between bites of steak and kidney pud, I described the morning.

"The worse thing is, they're afraid of me," I said. "They do what I ask them, but they won't make eye contact with me."

Jack nodded. "They'll be over it in a couple days, especially when they see it's best for the business and for them."

"But that's the thing!" I exclaimed. "I don't know that it is."

"Of course, it is. That girl would have brought down the whole salon eventually, especially if she kept letting clients down."

"She did, but Rose ended up taking on most of her clients. Rose took the ones who wouldn't reschedule, they took a liking to her, and we ended up retaining them."

I took a breath. "And since she's not there anymore, it falls on the rest of us to answer the phone and make the tea and such."

Jack pressed my hand. "You're down a junior; things are bound to be hectic for a bit. Until you take on another junior, that is." He paused. "I assume there are other newly qualified hairdressers in London?"

His blue eyes were narrowed in amusement, and a little laugh escaped me.

"Oh, we'll find a replacement, eventually. But in the meantime, things will be a nightmare, and what about Emmy?"

"What about her?"

"Her job prospects! Other salons will wonder why I let her go."

Jack shrugged. "Mandy, you'll write her a perfectly adequate reference. If she's as personable as you say she is, she'll talk herself into another situation."

I stared at the remains of my pud. "I hope so."

Once again, his hand rested on mine. Strong fingers massaged my knuckles.

"Chin up, Mandy," said Jack softly. "The first time is always the hardest. It'll come off all right; you'll see."

He meant well, bless him.

"I talked to my friend Elsie last night," I said in my usual voice. "Her book is coming out next month, and she'd like us to go to her book launch in Regent's Park."

Jack's hand pressed mine. "Lovely. I'd like to meet your friends."

"Oh, Elsie's a sweetheart, you'll love her. She's American. She's married to Alec, one of Dave's old bandmates."

The hand stiffened.

"Dave won't be at the launch," I said quietly.

Jack smiled, and his hand relaxed.

Of course, I reflected, I didn't know anything of the sort. Elsie and Alec had remained friends with both of us after the divorce, so it was possible Dave might be there.

Something else must have occurred to Jack because his brow was furrowed.

"I assume this will be a respectable affair," he said. "No drugs or anything of the sort."

I giggled. Sometimes, Jack could be so funny.

"Oh, nothing like that. Alec's rock 'n' roller days are behind him. That is, he's got his own band, but I don't think he ever has more than a couple pints on the road. And I don't think Elsie's ever touched a drug in her life, bless her."

Now Jack raised his eyebrows. "Is that so strange then? Not taking drugs?"

"No. Just surprising, I guess. Because of when we were young."

Then I remembered that Jack was fifty. He wasn't young when we were young.

He was staring at me, and I gulped. I felt like a teenager who'd been caught smoking.

I sighed. "I first qualified as a hairdresser in 1968, Jack. I shared a flat in Camden with a few other girls, and one night, one girl's boyfriend brought some cannabis for us to try."

One hand around his pint, Jack gestured for me to continue with the other. "And?"

"I tried some," I said defiantly. "I'd never laughed so much in my life."

He was still staring at me.

"So after that, my flatmate Melanie and I decided we wanted more," I continued. "For about a week, we smoked every night and more on the weekend.

"Then, that Tuesday, I went into work in a haze. I wondered why one client was looking daggers at me, and then I realized it was because I'd asked her twice if she was going anywhere nice on holiday."

Jack's features relaxed into a smile. "And that was the end of it?"

"Yes. Oh, I'd take a toke at a party now and then, but I never got high properly."

"And there was no cocaine or LSD or anything of that sort, I take it?"

"No. I took speed once, but I didn't like it." I paused. "I suppose Elsie and I are disappointing as rock musicians' wives or ex-wives."

He smiled. "Hardly." But I knew he was relieved.

The afternoon was nearly as hectic as the morning. When I left the salon, I shivered in the January evening. I couldn't face cooking, so I decided to pick up some ready-made meals at the Marks and Spencer in Kensington.

I selected macaroni cheese. It would be easy to heat up, and there would be no complaints from Katie or Sam.

"Mandy? Is that you?"

A tall woman with feathered dark hair stood behind me. She wore a camel-colored wool duffle coat, and she was attractive in a hard sort of way.

"Betty!" I exclaimed. "It's brilliant to see you."

I hadn't seen Betty, the ex-wife of Serval's singer, since Dave and I divorced five years earlier. Betty and Greg's marriage had broken up around the same time just as the band itself was dissolving.

Her face softened. "It's been ages, hasn't it? And we meet again in the food section of all places."

"Listen," I said. "I've got to get back to Ealing to serve this to the kiddies, but I've got time for a drink if you do. A half."

She hesitated.

"My treat," I said.

Her face broke into a smile, and suddenly she looked years younger. "Thanks, Mandy."

We ducked into the Goat Tavern just down the street, ordered half pints of lager, and found a little table near the window.

"I saw your salon in the *Evening Standard*," said Betty. "You've made a good go of it—well done."

"I wouldn't have made the *Standard* if I hadn't been Dave's ex-wife."

"But you own a salon in the King's Road. If that's not success, I don't know what is."

She opened a packet of cigarettes and offered me one.

I shook my head. "I've given up, thanks."

"Good for you." Betty lit one and exhaled to the side. "I should do. I would if I had willpower."

"It's hard. Giving up took me forever."

I asked about her son, Jason.

"Oh, he's fifteen and knows just about everything." But her pride showed in her face.

"Mad how fast they grow."

"How old are yours?"

"Katie's seven, and Sam's ten."

She smiled. "I remember them as babies."

Suddenly, her smile vanished. "How is Dave with maintenance?" she asked quietly.

"Fine. He pays his share on time and takes them every other week."

"Good for you."

That meant Greg wasn't reliable. I waited for her to elaborate.

Studying the table, she flicked ash from her cigarette.

"Greg has reinvented himself as a lounge singer," she said. "He goes to places like Weymouth and Weston-super-Mare and sings big band songs to the old girls. It doesn't pay that well, and most of what he earns is spent at one pub or another."

"I'm sorry," I said because I couldn't say anything else.

"Of course, it turns out that I don't need much maintenance," said Betty meditatively. "I've remarried, you see—a bloke I knew at school—and even though he's on the dole, he's capable of meeting most of my needs. And Jason's."

"That's not fair!"

Amusement flickered in Betty's dark eyes.

"I never thought life would be, not even when I married Greg. I could put up with the women and the drink, but I never anticipated poverty."

She laughed. "I've sold most of the jewelry Greg bought me when we were married and the chinchilla coat. I shouldn't be entering the food section at Marks and Sparks, let alone spending my money on readymade meals. By all rights, it should be bangers, mash, and tinned beans from Tesco every night."

All I could do was change the subject.

"Do you ever hear from Irene?" I asked. She had always gotten on well with the bassist's wife.

"I get a card at Christmas. Did you know she's remarried?"

"I didn't."

"When she and Billy split up, she hired a solicitor."

I nodded. That's what you did when you wanted a divorce.

"Well, she cried a lot then even though she was the one who wanted a divorce. She still loved Billy even with his cocaine habit and his womanizing. She could forgive him his cheating until it followed him home."

I raised my eyebrows.

"Yes, some blonde he'd met on the road knocked on her front door and introduced herself to Irene as Billy's girlfriend."

"Poor girl." As bad as Dave was, at least that hadn't happened.

"But apparently, Mr. Chelmsford, her solicitor, was a nice man, a bit older than she was. Very attentive. All of a sudden, Irene realized she was still young and quite attractive. And so six months after her divorce from Billy was final, she married Mr. Chelmsford."

"Really?"

"Yes, they've got a nice place in Middlesex, not far from where she and Billy used to live."

"Good for her." I paused. "What kind of a stepfather is he?"

"Oh, Mr. Chelmsford adores Jill. And the feeling is mutual. She has no time for Billy anymore."

"What?"

"Miss Jill now calls Mr. Chelmsford 'Daddy.' Apparently, she's very cold to Billy during their visits."

"Poor Billy," I said faintly. "I always liked him."

"Me, too," said Betty thoughtfully. "Though I don't know why."

"I know he wasn't a perfect father," I began, "but he loved Jillian. He bought her that pony—"

"Oh, they've still got Clover," said Betty. "Mr. Chelmsford has a nice little padlock on his property, and Jill's doing very well in Pony Club."

"And Billy?" Apart from Alec, Dave hadn't kept up with his former bandmates, at least as far as I knew.

"Last I heard, he'd had to go on the dole because he couldn't get enough work as a session musician. Good thing Irene doesn't need maintenance."

"It's funny, isn't it?" I said. "Irene was the one I always worried about. Back when we were all married."

Betty lit another cigarette. "Yes, she always seemed so fragile. She and little Elsie. How is Elsie by the way?"

"Brilliant. She's got a book coming out next month."

"Good for her. I always liked her. I hope Alec's good to her."

"They're happy. I think they have been. Mostly."

She shrugged. "Mostly's all we can ask for. I am with Nat, mostly. And you?"

"Am I happy? I suppose so. I've just had to sack a junior, though—" Suddenly, a thought occurred to me.

"How would you like to be a salon receptionist?" I asked.

Twelve

Two days later, Betty started at Luxor.

She was sleek and elegant in her sateen blue blouse with a cravat and black leather jacket, but she smiled a little nervously when she shook hands with Robbie and Rose. It was understandable. She hadn't worked since her son was born fifteen years earlier, shortly before Serval had taken off in earnest.

"Thank you for coming to look after us," said Rose in her quiet way.

"Oh, absolutely, we need to be kept in line," said Robbie airily. "We need a matron or a headmistress at the very least."

Betty laughed. "I'll see what I can do."

I let Rose show her the diary and the tea things, while Robbie explained the intricacies of scheduling: how much time to allot for a trim, permanent, cut, and color. Of course, I could have set her straight, but I wanted her to get on with Robbie and Rose, and this seemed the easiest way to have them get to know each other.

Though the morning was a busy one, I occasionally peeked at the front desk. At first, Betty greeted customers and answered the phone a little stiffly, but within a couple hours, she was relaxed and smiling. Her face was losing the pinched look it had had when we met in the food section. Once again, she was the tall, poised girl who had been a shop assistant at one of the smartest shops in the King's Road and then married a rock singer. Cool, yet approachable, she was just who I wanted at the front desk.

Best of all, Rose and Robbie seemed more lighthearted than they had since I'd sacked Emmy. Even if they still felt for Emmy, they no longer seemed to resent me. There were snatches of banter between clients, and they included Betty and me in their conversations.

That day, Jack and I were having lunch at the pub across the road. He met me at Luxor, where I made a point of introducing him to Betty.

"Jack, this is Betty Steves, our new receptionist," I said. "Otherwise known as a lifesaver. Betty, this is Jack Slayton." His role in my life seemed obvious.

"Pleasure." Jack shook her hand, and he and I left Luxor hand in hand.

Soon, we were settled in a corner booth, glasses of cabernet sauvignon and chardonnay in our hands.

"So, a new receptionist."

"Yes. She's just begun today and already my life is much easier."

"Oh?"

"Robbie and I don't have to make tea or sweep hair between clients, and Rose is getting so many of her own clients these days that we can't always spare her to answer the phone or make tea."

Over the rim of his glass, steely blue eyes peered at me. "What about your plan to take on another junior?"

"Oh, yes." I hesitated. "I would have done eventually, only I ran into Betty at Marks and Sparks."

Put that way, it sounded like a very silly decision. Jack seemed to think the same thing for his eyebrows met in a frown.

"We hadn't seen each other in years," I continued. "Since I split up with Dave, in fact. Her ex-husband, Greg, was Serval's lead singer. We had a drink at a pub just around the corner, and it came out that she was in a bad way. Greg's rubbish about paying maintenance, and her husband's on the dole. It occurred to me that she could help with the salon, and so I offered her a job."

Jack set down his drink. "So you gave her the job because you felt sorry for her." His voice was quiet, probing.

"No." I flushed. "Well, yes and no. Yes. I felt sorry for her. Who wouldn't? But you can't deny I needed help at Luxor."

Jack sighed. "But what kind of help can this woman give you, Mandy? What are her skills, her experience, her qualifications?"

"She's personable, presentable, and reliable," I snapped. "Isn't that enough for a salon receptionist?"

"But what experiences prepare her to work at your salon? Being a rock musician's ex-wife?"

He'd never been this sarcastic before.

"She was a shop assistant at a very fashionable boutique in the King's Road before she had her son," I said hotly. "She has poise. She could have been a model."

"But that was years ago, Mandy. And what will she do for the salon's image? She must be forty—"

"She's thirty-six!" I exclaimed. "Two years older than I am." And fourteen years younger than you, I might have added.

"She doesn't look like you, Mandy." He paused. "You need someone young and trendy at the desk. One, if not the other. She's over thirty-five, and she lacks the means to project the image you want."

"It's not her fault her bloke's on the dole!" I said. "And you can't say she's not fashionable. Not with the blouse and jacket she's wearing."

"No," admitted Jack.

"She's capable of looking smart on the dole," I said. "Think how she'll look after a few weeks' wages. And Robbie and Rose are delighted with her. She's already got the punters eating out of her hand."

Jack studied me carefully. Then he smiled.

"Well, you know your business better than I do," he replied. "And if you think this woman is an asset and not a risk, then I accept it."

"She is most definitely an asset. And if there is to be another Luxor, I'll need a receptionist in that salon, too."

Jack laughed. "Touché, Mandy."

The barmaid brought our sandwiches, and we talked of other things.

That afternoon, the last client on Robbie's schedule was a David Drummer.

Betty and I were at the front desk when he entered. Behind his mustache, he smiled sheepishly at me.

"Good afternoon, Mr. Drummer," I said. "Or is that Mr. Wilt?"

"You saw through my ruse this time," replied Dave. "Nice one, Mandy." A finger toyed with his moustache, but his blue eyes laughed into mine.

"Oh, my God, Dave, I didn't recognize you," said Betty. "You all right?"

"Hello, Betty, I didn't know you worked here."

"I've only just started—"

"Good afternoon, Mr. Drummer," said Robbie languidly, sidling up beside me. "Or is that Mr. Davies? In any case, come through to the back."

After they left, Betty glanced sharply at me. "Davies?"

"The last time—the first time—he booked a haircut at Luxor, he scheduled an appointment for a Dave Davies. Robbie and I were expecting a Welshman. When Dave turned up, I remembered his mother was Welsh."

"Strange he didn't book it under Wilt this time," said Betty. "He's going through a lot of trouble with aliases."

She stifled a smile, and I began to be annoyed with her. Then my last client arrived, and I escorted her to my chair.

The client only wanted a quick trim, and she was out the door before Robbie finished Dave's cut. I was tidying up around my station when Dave approached.

I first caught sight of him in the mirror. Our eyes met, and I smiled.

"Happy with Robbie's handiwork?" I asked lightly, rearranging some potions.

"Yes. He's a nice bloke, and he does a good job."

"Is that why you returned to us?" I looked down and began to sweep the locks of hair around my station. Rose and Betty had enough to do; there was no reason I couldn't do some sweeping now and then.

"Yes. Partly."

I raised my eyes, and he lowered his for a second.

"Glad you like Luxor," I said. "We appreciate your patronage."

"How long has Betty been working here?"

"She only started today though you'd never know it; she's doing so brilliantly."

He nodded. "I didn't remember you having a receptionist the first time I came."

"I didn't. But I had to sack a junior earlier this week—"

Dave winced. "Oh, that's awful. I remember when we had to do that with someone on the crew."

I frowned. "I don't remember that story."

"I probably didn't tell you. Think it was around 76, maybe 77. There was a roadie named Bob who would just disappear during shows. We'd tried giving him second and third chances, but it didn't work."

"Who sacked him?" I asked. It was hard to imagine any of the members of the band dismissing someone.

Dave laughed ruefully and stuck his hands in his back pockets. "It was supposed to be all four of us confronting Bob. But Greg chose to hide in some pub all day, and when it came to it, Billy couldn't do it. He used to do coke with Bob, and he felt as though he would be betraying him."

"So it fell to you and Alec."

"Just Alec. I backed out at the last minute." He paused. "So you're more of a manager than I've ever been."

"I'm not sure that's true. And if it is, I don't know if it's anything to be proud of."

"Anyway, how did you hire Betty?"

I described our meeting in the food section and our drink afterward.

"It just seemed like the right thing to do," I finished. "She needed the income, and I needed the help."

Dave's blue eyes were oddly luminous.

"You're a softie," he said quietly.

He raised a hand to my face and quickly withdrew it.

For a few seconds, we stared at each other and then the floor, unsure of what to say. The touch of his fingers lingered on my cheek. I could hear Robbie and Rose bantering in the backroom and Betty shuffling papers at the front desk.

Dave cleared his throat.

"Care for a drink? I know you've got to get back to Ealing, but we could get a half at the pub across the way."

The very spot where I'd had lunch with Jack that afternoon.

"I'm sorry," I said hurriedly, "but I've got to get back to Ealing. Mrs. Jones will be fed up if I leave the kids with her too long."

Dave nodded. "We can't try Mrs. Jones's patience," he said lightly. "Well, goodbye, Mandy. See you next week."

Next week? Surely, he wouldn't return for a trim so quickly. His hands returned to his pockets, he strode past the front desk, called goodbye to Betty, and stepped into the street.

Oh, yes. It was his turn to have the kids next weekend. I would spend those nights with Jack. Our nights together were a rare treat. Grown-up time, as Jack himself would say.

Thirteen

Over the next few days, Butler's appetite fluctuated. Dwindled, really. He'd eat almost normally one day, and then the next, I'd feel lucky if I could coax him to eat a few bites of wet food out of my hand.

I spent much of that weekend sat on the bedroom floor. Butler hid under the bed most of the day, but occasionally I coaxed him out. His little sandpaper tongue would lap gravy from my fingers. Afterwards, he'd settle near me, his hind leg looped over my arm as if to say, "She's mine."

He was always all boy.

Katie and Sam, bless them, were good about the weekend at home. Katie practiced her piano and then read her books and played with her dolls in her room. Sam met a friend at the park for a kickabout. But both of them joined me in my vigil. Sometimes together, sometimes alone, they insisted on keeping Butler and me company.

"Do you want me to grab Butler for you?" asked Katie on Saturday afternoon. She sat cross-legged beside me on the carpet, regarding me with her large blue eyes. "I could squeeze under the bed and get him."

Sam's brows knit together. "That would scare him!" he snapped. "How would you like it if someone just grabbed you when you were sick?"

Katie's lower lip trembled. "B-but I love Butler," she spluttered. "I would never hurt him." Her eyes grew moist.

I squeezed her shoulders. "There, there. We know you love Butler."

I shot Sam a look. "Your sister meant well."

Grimacing, he crossed his arms.

I rolled my eyes. Even at a time like this, they could fight.

Jack and I had planned dinner on Saturday night—Mrs. Jones from next door had agreed to look after the kids—but I rang him that afternoon.

"I'm sorry, Jack," I said, "but I can't go out tonight. Butler's really bad."

"I thought he was eating a bit more."

"Oh, he'll perk up one day, and then the next, I'll be lucky if I can get him to eat a tablespoon of his food."

"I'm sorry, Mandy." Jack paused. "But surely it wouldn't hurt to leave him for a couple hours. I mean, no harm can come to him with the neighbor next door. Or she could even stay at yours with the children."

I sighed. "I'm sorry, Jack. I just can't. We've been through a lot together, Butler and me. I need to do this for him."

"But aren't you taking him to the vet?"

"On Tuesday." My stomach twisted. Put like that, it sounded far off.

"You're very fond of that cat."

I wasn't sure if this was a criticism or an observation.

"I love him," I said quietly.

Once again, there was a pause on the other end of the line.

"All right, Mandy," he said. "You do what you need to do. Let's plan on Tuesday night, then."

I nodded, then remembered he couldn't see me. "Of course."

"Well, see you. I love you, Mandy,"

"I love you."

Replacing the receiver, I realized I didn't want Tuesday to come.

But arrive it did. Butler ate a bit more on Monday, and he even used his scratching post. So even though he was slight and lethargic, I hoped he might be getting better.

On Tuesday morning, I pulled him out from under the bed. As I placed him in his carrier, I was struck by his lightness. He'd once been a sturdy cat—slightly overweight, according to the vet—but now he seemed to weigh little more than a kitten. And while normally he would do anything to avoid the carrier, which he associated with the vet, today, he was passive.

I kept up a steady stream of chatter as I drove to the vet's surgery in Northfields.

"We're going to see Dr. Greyson," I said brightly. "You remember him? He's given you your shots and weighed you and poked and prodded you for the past five years. Before that, you had Dr. Watson, so your dad always said, 'Elementary, my dear Watson,' whenever you had an appointment."

And I went on in that vein until I parked the Cavalier in front of Dr. Greyson's surgery.

In the waiting room, I sat on a chair with a red seat. A few chairs away, a man sat with his liver and white spaniel, who kept straining at his leash and barking. Why did he keep a gun dog in London?

Opposite us, an old lady in a kerchief held a chihuahua on her lap. Whenever the spaniel barked, the poor little thing trembled.

I held Butler's carrier on my lap and murmured to him. "Now these dogs are just as scared as you are, only they've got a funny way of showing it."

"Mrs. Wilt? Dr. Greyson will see you now."

Dr. Greyson's veterinary nurse, a stout fair girl with a broad face, was standing and smiling at us. I rose from my seat and followed her.

The exam room was white and sterile except for the steel sink. It smelled of antiseptic and fear, and I hated it.

Dr. Greyson entered the room through another door. In his fifties, he was balding, and behind his glasses, his green eyes were kind.

"How's Butler today?" he asked. I recognized his rehearsed cheerfulness. It was the voice I used when I didn't feel like cutting someone's hair.

"He's lost a lot of weight, and he's not eating," I said all in a rush. "Well, he's not eating or drinking much. He'll eat a bit more one day, then hardly anything the next."

The nurse pulled Butler from his carrier and set him on the scale. "2.72 kilograms," she murmured.

Dr. Greyson's long fingers palpated Butler's belly. "Some swelling in the abdomen. How long has this been going on, Mrs. Wilt?"

I opened my mouth, then shut it. "I—I hardly know. Over the past month, his appetite has just declined."

They didn't look at me, Dr. Grayson or his nurse. She held Butler while he continued to palpate him. Still, I felt them judging me. But the worst was Butler's green eyes, large and terrified, looking beyond me at something I couldn't see.

I'd been a fool—worse than a fool—not to bring him weeks earlier.

Finally, Dr. Greyson's eyes met mine. When he spoke, his voice was gentle.

"Mrs. Wilt," he began, "Butler has a very fast-growing tumor in his abdomen. I could do a blood test or x-rays, but I'm not sure they'd tell us anything we don't already know."

"You mean he has cancer," I said stupidly.

Dr. Greyson studied me carefully. "Yes, a very fast-growing cancer of the stomach, I should say."

I sank into the folding chair behind me. "I should have come in weeks ago," I said faintly.

"I'm not sure it would have made much difference, Mrs. Wilt. Once a tumor has metastasized, surgery is useless."

I stared at him. "You mean you can't do anything now?"

Now his voice was gentler than ever.

"I'm afraid not, Mrs. Wilt. You may want to consider euthanasia. He's never going to be a healthy cat, and he may suffer more if you prolong your decision."

My voice broke. "Can I—can I have a few moments alone with him? Just to think it over?"

"Of course."

I didn't see them leave the room, but they must have done. I stood next to the exam table and put an arm beside Butler. He looped his hind leg over my arm as he had done so many times before. I stroked the silky white fur on his head with one finger, and he purred.

He had given me his answer.

When Dr. Greyson knocked on the door, I kissed Butler's forehead one last time.

"Come in," I said, but there was a catch in my voice.

Later, I went to Luxor. I'd rescheduled all my appointments that day, but there was always something to do at the salon. And, in any case, work was better than being alone.

"Oh, my god, Mandy, are you all right?" asked Betty when I stepped through the door. Her dark eyes were wide with concern.

"It's Butler," I replied. Once again, my voice broke.

Somehow, she was in front of me, and her arms were around me.

"I'm sorry, love," she said. "That never gets easier."

Funny how comforting the scent of tobacco and Charlie perfume could be.

I stepped away and tried to laugh.

"What an image for Luxor!" I said lightly. "I don't know if the ancient Egyptians cried much about their cats, but they must have done. If they mummified them."

I spent the afternoon in the back, ordering supplies and looking at our accounts. Betty brought me a cup of tea, and to my surprise, Rose and Robbie found pretexts for going in the back.

About two hours after I arrived, Rose entered the back office, bearing a steaming cup of tea.

"I thought you might like another cuppa," she said, setting it on the desk before me.

"Thanks, Rose, that's lovely."

Uncertainly, she stood before me, one hand clasping the other. I'd forgotten how shy she could be. I smiled encouragingly at her.

"I just want to say that I'm sorry," she said. "About Butler. We had to—to do the same with one of our cats last year, and it was awful."

"Thanks, Rose." I paused. "What was your cat's name?"

"Daisy. She was all black, but with a white chest and paws."

"A tuxedo. She must have been a beauty."

"She was."

She smiled then. "I have to go. I've got a client coming in a few minutes."

"Well, cheers for the tea, love."

As I inhaled the tea's aroma, it occurred to me that it was the best conversation we'd had since I sacked Emmy a week earlier. Things had gotten better after Betty started, but this was the first time we'd spoken normally to each other.

Not long after, Robbie appeared. When I raised my head from the account book, he lifted one sculpted eyebrow.

"I'm just looking for some extra capes," he said.

"You know where they are."

Out of the corner of my eyes, I watched him pull them from the wardrobe. When he addressed me, his back was toward me.

"Betty told me about Butler," he said. "I'm sorry."

"Thanks," I said. "I expect I'll miss him for some time. We had almost fourteen years together."

"You know, I had a dog when I was a wee boy," said Robbie, still rummaging in the wardrobe. "A little moggie. Terrier mostly. He was nothing to look at, bless him, but he was smart. My sister and I taught him all kinds of tricks. And he knew when I was due to come home from school. He'd wait for me at the front of the house."

Robbie paused. More was coming.

"Then, one day, I was on me way home from school. I must have been ten, maybe eleven. I could see him waiting for me. But then he saw a cat on the pavement across the street. He raced into the road."

"The lorry driver could have stopped in time, but he didn't."

"Oh, Robbie, I'm so sorry." Tears formed again in my own eyes.

"I cried all that afternoon until my dad came home. He told me only women and girlies cried over a dog. But when the tears kept flowing, he gave me a walloping."

"Robbie, I—"

He turned then, and though his green eyes were moist, his voice was as flippant as ever. "We really need a better place to store our capes, Mandy darlin'."

He sauntered out of the office, and I cried for Butler and for Daisy and the dog from Belfast.

Around four, I called Jack.

"I'm sorry," I said, "but I can't have dinner tonight. Butler—Butler's gone."

"Oh, Mandy, I'm sorry." Jack's voice was quietly concerned.

"I'm afraid I'm not much company at the moment. And I need to be with Katie and Sam tonight. This is the first time anything like this has ever happened to them."

"I understand." He paused. "Could I come round this evening? I'd bring takeaways for you and the kids. At least, you wouldn't have to cook."

"Oh, that's lovely." He was so thoughtful.

"My pleasure. I'll come round at around seven or so."

When I arrived home, I took the kids into the front room and asked them to sit on the sofa. Their eyes were large and curious as I sat in the chair opposite them. I hated what I had to say.

"You know how Butler has been very sick?" I began.

They nodded, and something in Sam's eyes made me think he knew what was coming.

"I took him to the vet, and it seems Butler had cancer. He was very, very sick."

Sam looked down. He knew.

"He was suffering, and he would only suffer more," I continued. "So Dr. Greyson and I decided to—to help him go to sleep. So he wouldn't suffer anymore."

I held Katie close, her small body shaking as she sobbed. Sam tried not to cry, and though I was touched to see him try to play the man, I remembered Robbie's story.

I sat on the floor beside Sam and squeezed his hand. "It's all right to cry," I whispered. "It means you loved Butler."

Though his dark eyes were filled with tears, he tried to smile at me. I almost jerked my head back. He looked like Dave then. Or how Dave had looked the few times I'd seen him cry.

An hour later, the doorbell rang. It was Jack with the takeaway curries. He set down the bag and held me close. His wool coat smelled of his Kouros. It felt good to be held and loved after the day I'd had.

I expected him to say, once again, that he was sorry about Butler, but he didn't.

"Before we tackle the curries, I've just got one thing in the car."

As he stepped outdoors, I wondered what it could be. Had he brought me a present or something for the kids?

He reentered, bearing a wrapped box topped with a large red bow. "Let's open this before we eat," he declared.

"All right," I said dully. I could have murdered some naan bread, but it was sweet of him to bring a gift.

I followed him into the front room.

"Hi, Katie, hi, Sam," he said.

They said hello politely.

"I've got something for you," he said brightly.

His eyes smiled into mine. "All of you, that is."

He set down the parcel and removed the top with its bow. Tiny mews escaped the box.

The kids were beside it in an instant. Soon, Katie and Sam were holding kittens, one yellow and one white. They had long hair and flat little faces and large, innocent blue eyes. When the kids set them down, they wrestled with each other and then purred when the kids picked them up again.

I couldn't believe it. I sank onto the loveseat and stared.

"Like them, Mandy?" Jack was beside me, holding my hand.

"Oh, yes, they're very sweet," I said faintly.

"Persian," he said. "I rang a pet shop in Camden, and they just happened to have two kittens left in the litter. I couldn't have planned it better."

Certainly, Katie and Sam seemed delighted with them. You'd never have guessed that they'd been crying their eyes out about Butler an hour earlier. But they were kids after all.

I planted a kiss on Jack's cheek. "You've very sweet, you know."

His eyes were soft. As he returned my kiss, it occurred to me that he didn't understand at all.

Fourteen

The kids named the kittens Lemon Drop and Peppermint. Or rather, Katie did.

"Lemon Drop's a rubbish name for a boy," snorted Sam over his Cheerios the next morning.

"It suits him," replied Katie in a faraway voice. "And Peppermint suits Peppermint." She paused. "And if Peppermint's too long, we can always call her Minty."

Minty Paige was about my least favorite client. I shuddered involuntarily as I raised my coffee cup to my lips.

"See? Mum agrees with me with me," said Sam forcefully. "It's a stupid name for a cat."

Katie's blue eyes began to fill with tears, and her lower lip trembled.

I rubbed her shoulder. "There, there, darling. Sam didn't mean it."

Then I turned to Sam. "I don't think Peppermint and Lemon Drop are silly names at all. Nor is Minty. I just reacted the way I did because I know someone called Minty."

Instantly, Katie's eyes were on my face. "What's the real Minty like, Mummy?"

"Well, she's very pretty," I began. "She's tall and blonde. She looks like a model."

Now, Katie's eyes were sparkling. Clearly, I would have to make her understand that the Minty I knew wasn't someone to look up to.

"She thinks very well of herself," I continued severely. "She edits a big magazine and walks around with her nose in the air."

Katie studied me intently. "Is editing a magazine better than having a salon, Mummy?"

"I suppose so," I replied. "Most people seem to think so. If it's a big magazine."

"Then why shouldn't Minty think well of herself?" Katie asked. "She looks like a model and edits a big magazine."

Put that way, it was pretty logical.

Now, eyes dark with anger, Sam slammed down his spoon. "But she didn't start a business from scratch like Mum did. Someone else runs it for her. It's nothing compared to what Mum's done."

He was ever my little champion, that one. I bit back a laugh and put my hand on his.

"Thanks, love, that's one of the nicest things anyone's ever said to me," I said softly. "Now you two eat your breakfast before you're late for school."

So all week, Lemon (Lemon Drop proved too long in the end) and Minty warmed our laps, play fought, and scaled the front room curtains. They were sweet, and I had to admit that Minty Paige's namesake was nothing like her. No doubt the kitten knew she was our superior, but unlike the editor, she was disposed to be pleased with us. In any case, it was nice to have the kittens in the house, and it warmed my heart to see the kids play with them.

But they weren't Butler.

At Luxor, things had improved a great deal. It was pleasant to have someone take charge of the phone and the tea things, and since Betty never called in, Robbie, Rose, and I could concentrate on our clients. I began to think I could handle two salons—if I had a Betty at the helm of each of them, that is.

And on Friday morning, Robbie gave me some news that lifted my spirits.

As ever, we were the first in the salon. When I entered, he greeted me in the usual way with raised eyebrows.

"Hello, Robbie, you all right?" I asked brightly. Although we'd gotten on better ever since I'd hired Betty and lost Butler, things still weren't quite as they used to be, and I felt an obligation to be friendlier than usual.

"All right, Mandy darlin'." He paused. "You'll never guess who I saw at the pub last night."

"Terrance?" He'd seen a bloke called Terrance a few times in the autumn, and though he'd not admitted as much, I knew he'd been gutted when Terrance had stopped ringing.

"Nothing so obvious, darlin.' Emmy."

My face grew hot and my palms sweaty. The girl was probably drowning her sorrows in cheap wine. Mostly to occupy my hands, I foraged for my lipstick in my handbag.

"Is she all right?" I asked casually as I opened my lipstick case.

"Oh, she's more than all right. She's got a chair at a salon in Fulham. One of her mates works there, and she got Emmy in."

"So quite a promotion, then," I replied, smiling. "She's a junior no more." I was happy for her and more than a little relieved.

Robbie raised one arched eyebrow. "Yes, you can go off to Bristol with a clear conscience, Mandy darlin'. You can say, in a way, that you were the making of her."

Without a word, I grabbed my bag and stalked to the toilet.

Robbie was right, of course, I reflected as I applied lipstick and adjusted my hair. I had felt guilty about Emmy, and now I felt as though a weight had been lifted from my shoulders. And while Chelsea might have been a more desirable location for a new stylist, she had, on the whole, gone up in the world.

Really, the Emmy affair had come off well. Funny that I'd hesitated so long before sacking her. Sacking people would never be enjoyable, but it was necessary sometimes, and I could do it if need be. And through hiring Betty, I had, quite by chance, discovered how indispensable a receptionist was to a salon. How naïve I had been to think I could manage with one other hairdresser and two juniors.

I knew, then, that I could run a salon. And if one was a success, it wasn't much of a stretch to think I could manage two.

That evening, Jack was taking me to Bristol for the weekend. I was taking Saturday off, and we were going to look at a site for Luxor II. Now, for the first time, I found myself as excited as he was at the prospect. Perhaps he had been right all along: the world needed another Luxor.

Dave had the kids that weekend, and since we hoped to reach Bristol in time for dinner, he came round earlier than usual to fetch them. I left work at four, and his Golf was parked out front by a quarter past five.

His hands were in his coat pockets as he stepped into the foyer. He stood awkwardly for a minute before speaking.

"You're off to Bristol, then?" he said, smiling.

"Yes, we're inspecting a property near the university. It's quite a trendy place, Clifton, and Jack thinks it'd be perfect for Luxor II."

"All very exciting."

I searched Dave's face, but there was nothing ironic in his expression or tone. He was pleasant, interested.

I felt I should reciprocate by showing interest in him.

"How's work for you?" I asked.

Instantly, I chided myself for asking the question. I knew he wasn't getting much session work at the moment.

"There isn't a terrible lot of it at the moment," he said. "Though I did get to play on an awful—"

At that moment, Minty raced in front of us with Lemon in hot pursuit. They wrestled in the middle of the floor before streaking off again.

"What was that?" Dave asked.

"Lemon and Minty," I said. "I'm sure the kids will tell you all about them. Jack brought them round on Tuesday evening."

"How's poor old Butler taking it all?"

My face must have told the truth because his blue eyes became concerned.

"I'm sorry, Mandy," he said gently. "He was a bit of all right."

"I took him to the vet on Tuesday," I said, my voice breaking. "He had a fast-growing cancer; Dr. Greyson said he would never get better—"

Dave sighed and shook his head. "That's awful. I remember when Bruiser's hips got too bad. You know, I haven't had the heart to get another dog since."

"You mean Bruiser's dead?" I exclaimed.

I remembered when Dave had brought Bruiser home as a little brown and black puppy. I'd worried how Butler, a full-grown cat, would react to a boisterous little pup. But after a brief adjustment period, the two had become fast friends. I had photos of the cat sleeping peacefully atop the huge Alsatian.

Now I was grieving for two animals.

"He was ten years old when the vet put him down two years ago, Mandy. He was a big dog."

"But I thought you gave him to a neighbor!" I cried.

I remembered how irritated—disgusted, really—I'd been when Sam had told me gravely that Bruiser had gone to live with a neighbor. It had seemed to confirm everything childish and irresponsible about Dave.

Dave frowned. "Oh, yes, I think I told the kids he'd gone next door."

"You didn't!" It was like him, utterly like him.

Dave's eyes grew large, and his mustache seemed to droop. He looked, for all the world, like a dog who'd been caught eating the upholstery.

"It was cowardly, I know. I guess I didn't want to upset them or make them cry though they did a bit anyway." He paused. "How did they take Butler?"

"I sat them down in the front room, told them the truth, and they cried. An hour later, Jack appeared with the kittens, and they were all smiles again."

Dave's smile was wry. "All we go through to shield the little blighters, and then it turns out they were tougher than we were all along."

I returned his smile, but tears filled my eyes.

"My poor girl." Dave put his hands on my shoulders and stepped toward me. I was vaguely aware of the smell of tobacco and his leather jacket as he pulled me toward him.

I suppose I should have stopped him, but I didn't think to. It all felt natural.

"Daddy! What are you doing to Mummy?"

I supposed we looked a little like guilty dogs as we stepped apart.

At the top of the stairs, Katie stood, her eyes narrow beneath her two ponytails. She held her head high like an actress playing a duchess.

"What are you doing, Daddy?" she asked in the same imperious little voice.

"Hello, sweetheart," said Dave casually. "I've come to fetch you, of course."

She came down then, and Sam followed, lugging his suitcase. Dave raced up the stairs to grab Katie's bag.

As I waved goodbye to them from the big bay window, I thought over my exchange with Dave. He understood how I felt about Butler. He knew you couldn't replace an animal the way you could a jumper or a car.

I wondered what would have happened if Katie hadn't appeared when she did.

Fifteen

The Bristol site was on the Queens Road, just past the university. It had been a salon, so the sinks and mirrors and chairs were already installed. The ceilings were high and the light from the front windows ample. In all respects, it was an ideal site for a salon.

"There wouldn't be much to do apart from the artwork," murmured Jack as we stood together at the salon's rear, surveying the interior. "You could get the same artist in to do the murals. The pharaohs and all."

"I could." I paused. "But I'm not sure about the sinks and chairs. It's not quite the look I had in mind for Luxor II."

Jack shrugged. "Install new ones once it's yours."

"Yes. But it's so small after the other salon."

Though my voice was barely above a whisper, I could swear that Mr. Willoughby, the estate agent, heard every word I uttered. He stood at the front of the salon, hands in his coat pockets, gazing out the window as though the comings and goings of the students at the café opposite were of paramount interest to him.

"This is Bristol, not London. You'd have fewer stylists, fewer punters."

"Let me have a think about it."

Smiling, Jack shook his head. He took my hand then, and together we went to face Mr. Willoughby.

At our approach, Mr. Willoughby turned, a smile frozen on his lips, his eyebrows lifted in anticipation.

Jack was the first to extend his hand. "Thanks for your time, Mr. Willoughby. We'll have a think on it."

"Yes, thanks for your time, Mr. Willoughby," I echoed.

Mr. Willoughby frowned. Then, recollecting himself, he formed his lips into a smile.

"It was a pleasure, Mr. Slayton, Mrs. Wilt. But mind you don't think too long. This part of Bristol is very sought-after."

Outside the salon, Jack stood in front of me. As his eyes met mine, I was struck again by their steely blueness. Though, at this moment, they were softer than usual, and little laugh lines appeared around them.

Jack put his arms around me.

"You're a perfectionist, Mandy. It's one of the things I love about you."

He bent his head and kissed me on the mouth in the middle of the Queens Road with shoppers and students streaming by us. As I returned his kiss, I wanted to say no, no, I'm not.

***

"So, how was Bristol?" asked Robbie on Tuesday morning as we prepared for the day.

"Lovely," I said. "We stayed at the Grand Hotel. On Saturday afternoon, we walked up to the Clifton Suspension Bridge. I'd not been to Bristol in ages, and I'd forgotten how nice it is even in the winter."

"And the future home of Luxor II?"

"The location was ideal: in Clifton near the university."

"And the digs themselves?"

"The place used to be a salon, so it's got all the sinks and mirrors and chairs. And a big front window with lots of light."

Robbie had been flipping through the salon's diary, but at that, he raised his head. "So you've made an offer or will very soon?"

"I said I'd think about it."

The left eyebrow spoke before Robbie himself did. "But a space like that will just vanish, darlin.' You've got to act quickly."

"That's what Jack said."

"Then why hesitate?"

I shrugged. "The chairs and sinks. I didn't quite like them."

Now Robbie was staring at me. "It'd be easy enough to swap them out."

"Jack said that."

"Then why not jump at it, Mandy darlin'?"

I rummaged in my bag for my lipstick. "It was small," I said, "Not quite my vision for Luxor II."

Out of the corner of my eye, I saw Robbie stare at me for another minute. Then his eyes returned to the diary.

"I sometimes wonder if any place will live up to your vision," he remarked lazily.

In a huff, I snatched my handbag and headed for the toilet.

The morning passed quickly. I was rather looking forward to lunch that day. My sister, Kate, was meeting me, and different though we were, I knew she would be sympathetic to our plans for Luxor. She'd always been business-minded, Kate, even as a girl.

My last client before lunch was new. When I saw her name in the diary, I didn't give it much thought. Our clientele was growing, and though new patrons were generally assigned to Rose, some were willing to wait for Robbie or me.

The second-to-last client before lunch only wanted a trim, so I was able to tidy up my station a bit before the new client, Cheryl Blake, arrived. I was surprised, then, when Betty stalked toward my station, her mouth set in a hard line.

"Cheryl's here," she said tightly.

"The new client. Tell her I'll be with her in just a minute."

"She's not new at all. Well, she is, but she's not a stranger."

She paused and then hissed in a whisper, "It's Cheryl Wiles."

Cheryl Wiles. She'd been a pop singer in the early seventies, and for about a year, she'd gone out with Alec, Serval's guitarist, before he met Elsie. She'd always had to be the center of attention, and we'd all been relieved when Alec split up with her.

Come to think of it, the last time I'd seen Cheryl, she'd been miserable to Elsie. I certainly never expected her to appear in my salon.

My jaw must have dropped because Betty gave a hard little smile.

"Oh, yes. She was delighted to see me. And glad I'd found something to do with my life now that I'm not married to Greg anymore. She'd been worried about me."

I grimaced. "Cheers for the warning, love."

A real smile flickered in Betty's eyes. I smoothed my dress and formed my lips into what I hoped was a welcoming expression.

Cheryl was flipping through an issue of *She* in the waiting area. At my approach, she rose, beaming.

"Mandy, it's fab to see you!" she cried. "You've not aged a day."

She embraced me as though we'd been close friends. I forced myself to return her hug.

"It's nice to see you, Cheryl. You're looking lovely yourself."

She did, too, for the most part. Petite and fair, she'd kept her figure well. Although she must have been about thirty-six, she could still pass for twenty-five in her short, belted green dress. Still, there was a hardness about her green eyes that stopped her from looking really young.

She laughed. "It's the touring that keeps me youthful, I expect. Anyhow, I knew you worked here, but I never expected a Serval reunion. It's so good of you to give Betty a job."

Without looking at Betty, I knew it took every ounce of willpower for her not to grimace or vomit.

"We're lucky to have her," I declared loudly. "I don't know where I'd be without her. Now do come through to the back."

Cheryl wanted a layered cut and a frost. She would. It would take ages.

As I colored, shampooed, and then cut her hair, Cheryl maintained a steady stream of chatter.

"Of course, I had to book an appointment with you after I saw the article in the *Evening Standard*, but like I said, I never expected to see Betty here. Do you keep up with the others?"

"Elsie and I are still close friends. Betty hears from Irene now and again."

"Irene!" Cheryl exclaimed as though they'd been bosom friends. "How is she?"

"She's doing well. She's remarried. A solicitor in Middlesex." I didn't mention his role in her divorce from Billy.

"Oh, yes, none of those marriages lasted, did they?" She sighed. "I suppose it's to be expected."

"Elsie and Alec are still together." I kept my voice and eyes expressionless.

Cheryl laughed a tinkling little laugh that would have been charming in any other woman.

"Oh, I didn't mean them. Though I suppose it was a bit different for them. I mean, I liked Elsie. I couldn't help liking her."

Since she'd only met Elsie once and had been particularly unpleasant to her on that occasion, I couldn't let that go. "You could have fooled me."

Once again, she gave her little bell-like giggle. "I'm not the jealous type, Mandy. And Elsie, bless her, didn't have a clue about what things are like on tour, being American and all."

My scissors were poised above her hairline. It would be so easy to remove all her fringe.

"I'm not sure being American has anything to do with it."

"Well, she was academic," said Cheryl, waving her hand airily. "She didn't know much about the real world—or what goes on on tour."

Her green eyes glittered as they met mine in the mirror. "Of course, none of the wives do."

I felt my face redden in spite of myself. Did she hope to hurt me by coming to my salon and throwing Dave's past in my face? I wouldn't give her the satisfaction.

"Anyhow," I said cheerfully. "Elsie's established herself as a writer. She's got a column in *Hearth and Home,* and she's published a novel. It's coming out next month."

Cheryl smiled smugly as though Elsie's accomplishments were laughable.

"I suppose it gives her something to do when Alec's away. Good for her."

It would be bad for the salon's reputation if I murdered a client with my shears.

"So what are you doing these days, Cheryl?" I asked in what I hoped was an even tone. She was always her favorite topic of conversation, so it seemed a safe choice.

Now she flashed me a brilliant smile in the mirror.

"Singing, touring. It never ends."

"Really? It's been ages since I heard you on the radio."

I shouldn't have said it, but I did. I had the satisfaction of seeing Cheryl's eyes flash green fire. But she quickly recovered her smile and her composure.

"You're obviously not listening at the right time, sweetie. My last single got loads of airtime. And my concerts sell out quickly. I've got big fanbases in Blackpool and Newcastle and Whitby."

That meant she played little holes in the wall in the winter and holiday camps in the summer. I smiled.

"You've got a beautiful voice, Cheryl. I'm glad you're still singing."

That much was true.

She flashed a smile at me. "And I'm glad Dave's still drumming. Many's the time I've been happy about his rhythm. And his licks."

There was something very strange about her voice and the way she smiled.

"But I always thought you toured with your own band, Cheryl. When Serval was still together."

Again, Cheryl laughed. "Yes, when Serval was together. But Dave's been part of my band since Serval split up."

My scissors paused in midair. In the mirror, Cheryl's reflection smiled smugly.

"He never said."

Her smile widened. "Oh, he never told you? I've been thankful to have a drummer of his caliber on the stage, and then there were the nights—"

She broke off and let the word sink in. I felt her eyes on my face.

"Bands usually go out for drinks after the show," I said evenly.

"Yes," she said airily. "And Dave and I always have plenty to talk about after the rest of the band go to bed."

Her green eyes studied me for a moment before she continued. "We've reminisced about old times, and we—well, let's just say we've made some new memories."

<h1 style="text-align:center">Sixteen</h1>

Somehow, I finished Cheryl's haircut. And if I wasn't as warm as I usually was when I showed clients their new look, I wasn't actually rude. I even smiled and said, "See you later," as she left Luxor.

In a trance, I slicked on bright pink lipstick and donned my coat.

"Are you all right, love?" asked Betty quietly as I crossed the lobby.

"Yes, thanks," I replied, opening the door. My voice sounded robotic even to my ears.

The cold air slapped my cheeks. I scrunched up my face as I walked into the wind. Now I would arrive red and pinched for my lunch with Kate. Brilliant.

When I arrived at the restaurant, Kate was already waiting at a table in a little conservatory just off the main dining room. She smiled slightly when I entered, even rising briefly to kiss my cheek.

"Hello, Kate. You're looking lovely."

She was, too. Three inches taller than I, she was as svelte as she'd been when Dave had paid her fees at the secretarial college thirteen years earlier. Her shoulder-length blonde hair was capped with a red

Alice band, and she sported a plaid skirt and red jumper. She wasn't a Sloane Ranger, but she didn't have the look of someone who needed to type for a living or do much of anything for that matter.

Kate acknowledged the compliment with another smile, revealing a fleeting glimpse of teeth whiter and more even than mine.

I'd always considered her the pretty one, but Dave had disagreed.

"She's got no figure for one," he'd said. "And for another, she's dull. Fancies herself too much to be much good to anyone. She's perfect for Jon."

"I ordered a bottle of chardonnay," Kate said. "The waiter's bringing it now."

"Is my need that obvious?"

The waiter appeared. After filling our glasses, he took our orders. When he left, Kate raised her glass. "Santé."

"Santé." I raised my glass and took a bigger sip than I should have. Then I coughed. God. Now my face would be redder than ever.

"How is Jon?" I asked hurriedly. Asking about her life seemed the best way to get the attention off me.

"Pretty snowed under at the moment. He's acquired another dealership, and he's sorting out the staff there."

I'd lost track of how many dealerships Kate and Jon owned. "So not much time for golf these days."

"Not in the winter."

Kate could always make me forget I was three years older and the owner of a moderately successful salon. "Of course, that was dull of me."

She acknowledged this with a smile.

I grasped for another question to ask her. "Have you been playing a lot of tennis, then?"

"I play doubles a few days a week at the tennis club while Jennifer's at school. The indoor courts are quite nice, and sometimes, Jon even joins me for mixed doubles if he can get away for a couple hours during the day."

It was hard to believe that Kate had grown up with a single mother in a council flat, that she'd been lucky Dave could pay her fees at the secretarial college, and that she'd been even luckier to obtain the post at the Copper family's original dealership. Of course, the son of the family, the scion of the dealership dynasty, had fallen in love with her, so she hadn't been a secretary for long. Since her marriage, she'd quickly become at home in the golf and tennis worlds.

I asked her about her daughter, Jennifer, and then our chicken salads arrived. When the waiter left, her green eyes appraised me.

"How are you?" she asked.

"All right," I replied.

I took a bite of salad before continuing. "Business is steady; I've had to sack a junior and hire a receptionist—do you remember Betty? From Serval days? She used to be married to the lead singer?"

Kate's nod conveyed indifference to Betty's past or present marital status and to Serval itself. Even when she was a teenager, she'd been unimpressed by my connections to the music world.

"Anyhow, I ran into her in the food section at Marks and Sparks the week before last. We ended up having a drink, and since she'd fallen on hard times, I offered her a job. She's doing brilliantly; clients love her."

I waited for Kate to comment. She didn't. She nibbled her chicken salad and looked back at me.

"Katie and Sam are doing well at school," I continued. "We lost Butler last Tuesday—the vet had to put him down."

"I'm sorry," said Kate. She did love her pets. That was one point in her favor.

"The kids cried a lot, but Jack came over with two Persian kittens that night, so they made a rapid recovery. Me not so much."

Kate's green eyes met mine over her wineglass. "He sounds quite keen."

"He is. He gave me this bracelet at Christmas, and he's always encouraging me to open another salon, a Luxor II. He's always showing me possible sites. In fact, we looked at a property in Bristol this weekend. The location was ideal—in Clifton, near the university—and since it was a salon, it's already kitted out with chairs and sinks and mirrors."

Now something like interest flickered in Kate's eyes. "And will you buy it?"

I hesitated. "We're thinking about it. You see, it's a bit small—"

Kate hid her smirk in a sip of chardonnay. I wanted to slap her.

"Have the kids met Jack?" she asked.

"The four of us have been to the cinema a couple times, and, of course, they were there when he brought the kittens round. Jack's good with them. He knows how to be friendly, but not too familiar."

"So everything's going well?"

"Yes."

"Then why did you say you needed a drink when you sat down?"

My face must have shown my dismay, for her smile became faintly triumphant.

My mouth opened and closed a couple times as I hesitated. Oh, hell. It might feel good to tell someone about it, and Kate was my little sister after all.

I sighed. "Do you remember a pop singer called Cheryl Wiles? She was pretty popular when you were a teenager?"

"Vaguely."

"Well, she came to Luxor today."

In a rush, it spilled out of me: Cheryl's romance with Alec, her behavior to Elsie the one time they'd met, her visit to Luxor, and what she'd implied about her relationship with Dave.

"And he's never even mentioned being in Cheryl's band!" I concluded.

A small smile flitted over Kate's lips as she snapped open her burgundy handbag and extracted a packet of cigarettes. She placed one carefully between her lips, still red despite the chicken salad, and lit it with a silver lighter.

Never an addictive smoker, she nonetheless had to have an elegant lighter. It was like her. And she never missed an opportunity to smoke in front of me.

"You're going to smoke just one."

"Yes."

"And you'll smoke it, enjoy it, and tap it out without thinking of when you'll light up again."

"Yes." Smoke drifted through her perfect lips.

"I bet you're the same way with biscuits. You'll eat one to be polite, perhaps two at Christmas."

"Yes."

"I hate you."

Now her smile was the widest and most sisterly it had been. "I know."

I should at least be thankful she had the decency not to offer me a cigarette.

"Anyhow, I can't understand why Dave wouldn't tell me he'd been part of Cheryl's band."

Kate shrugged. "Does he tell you about all his gigs?"

"No. To be honest, we hadn't spoken in person until this November. We'd just talk on the phone if we needed to talk about the kids."

"What changed then?"

"He came into the salon."

"To discuss the kids?"

"No. For a haircut."

For once in the thirty-one years Kate had been on Earth, I'd surprised her. "He booked a cut with you?"

"Yes. Well, under a different name. When I found out it was Dave, I gave him to Robbie. But we've talking more since. More often and more amicably. We have a chat when he comes round to fetch the kids." I didn't tell her he was becoming a regular at Luxor.

Kate's smile became very knowing. She tapped out her cigarette, her eyes downcast as though she had a private joke with the table or perhaps the ashtray.

"What is it? What's so funny?" Once again, we were ten and seven, two little girls sharing a room in a cramped flat, the younger one too knowing by half.

"You and Dave divorced five years ago, Mandy. Why should you care about Dave and some has-been?"

"But—"

"But what? You're going out with an attractive, successful man. What Dave does is no concern of yours—as long as the maintenance keeps coming."

"I . . . " I didn't know what to say, so the word hung in the air.

The waiter appeared. Kate paid him and then flashed her teeth at me.

"My treat. Listen, Mandy, I've got to run, but why don't you and Jack and the kids come to us in Middlesex sometime? It would be good for Jennifer to see her cousins, and Jon might have some ideas about your business plan. If you are ready to expand, that is."

Her lips touched my cheek, and she vanished before I could answer.

Seventeen

I n early February, Jack and I attended Elsie's book launch. It took place on a Thursday evening, and since Dave had the kids that weekend, he fetched them on Thursday instead of Friday.

I was wearing my black velvet dress with ruched sides when Dave stepped into the foyer, hands in his coat pockets.

"Hello, Mandy, you look nice." Then his eyes became large and sheepish like a dog who's aware he's done something wrong.

I kept a straight face. "Thanks. I wondered if you were going to Elsie's do."

"No, I was invited, but thought it'd be best—you know." His hands still in his pockets, he rocked back and forth on his heels. "I will buy a copy of Elsie's book, though."

"It's good."

"You've read it?"

"Not a printed copy. But she let me read a draft before she sent it to her editor. It's good."

It was, too, although it was nothing like the Dorothy Eden or Victoria Holt novels I usually chose when I had time to read. It was an odd little book about a woman and her cats. Literary, Elsie might say if she were talking about any book other than her own.

Dave nodded. "I'll read it."

I could tell that he was sincere; that is, that he would buy it even if he didn't read it, bless him. Considering he wasn't a reader, this meant a lot. It was sweet of him, and for a moment, I wanted to hug him for being so kind to Elsie. It was like him; he'd always been gentle with kids and old ladies and anyone he'd considered shy or vulnerable.

"That's really sweet of you," I said.

"Well, Elsie's a nice kid; I'd hate to let her down."

Then I remembered Cheryl's visit to Luxor. He couldn't say that he'd spent evenings with her because he felt sorry for her.

"Speaking of Serval days, I saw an old friend of yours recently," I said.

"Really? Who?" He sounded genuinely interested.

"Cheryl Wiles." I pronounced her name triumphantly.

Dave scowled. "Where'd you run into her?"

When you came right down to it, it was disgusting that he'd spent countless nights with the woman and then pretended to loathe her. It was just like a man.

"In Luxor. She booked a haircut."

"And who had the pleasure of cutting her tresses?"

"I did."

"Then I feel sorry for you. Awful woman. I remember her antics during our tour in 73."

He should have been an actor, that one.

"If you dislike her so much, then why are you in her band?" I was proud of myself for keeping my voice even.

Now his eyes were wide. "What?" he cried.

This was too much. "Oh, for God's sake, you've been part of her band for years!" I exclaimed. "Cheryl told me all about your shows up north and your nights out."

Puzzlement, then anger, flickered in his blue eyes. Then he laughed.

"What's so funny?" I snapped.

"Mandy, I played a few gigs with Cheryl in the summer of 82. A few little festivals and some small clubs up north. We were supposed to do more shows that summer and autumn. Then Cheryl realized she could dispense with a band as long as she had someone to back her on the synthesizer, so she dismissed her guitarist, bassist, and me and continued on with her keyboard player."

My mouth fell open. "So, you're not part of her band?"

"No. Cheryl can save a lot of money by just relying on a keyboard player. She has no interest in giving work to musicians. Any more than record companies do." Dave chuckled.

It did sound like Cheryl. But she'd sounded so smug when she'd alluded to their nights out.

"But she said the two of you went out for drinks—"

I remembered I had no right to question Dave about his social life.

"We all did," he said. "The whole band. Cheryl insisted on it. None of us wanted to, though, so it became a game to see who could sneak off first. One night, the guitarist and bassist left whilst I was in the gents. The keyboard player had a cold, so that left me alone with Cheryl. So I had another half with Cheryl and then called it a night. When she started sleeping with the keyboardist, things got easier for the rest of us—until we were out of a job."

Once again, Dave laughed. Then his eyes became thoughtful as he searched my face.

"Mandy, you didn't think—"

"Daddy!" called an imperious little voice.

Katie raced down the stairs and into his arms. Sam followed, lugging both of their bags.

"Goodbye, darlings," I said, kissing her cheek and then Sam's. "Bye, Dave. Enjoy the weekend—I've just got one more thing to do."

Without a backward glance, I trotted upstairs in my heels.

Jack picked me up in his Mercedes. He looked distinguished in his coat, and the scent of his spicy aftershave filled the car. It would be gratifying to walk into the bookseller on his arm.

"You look beautiful, Mandy." Jack's eyes smiled into mine as he grazed my fingers with his mouth.

I was glad he was coming to mine after the reading and the supper.

"So, who else is going to be at the reading tonight?" Jack asked.

"Besides Elsie and Alec? Some of her other friends, I suppose, and her editor and maybe Alec's mum. Her family couldn't fly in from America; her grandmother's very ill."

"I'm looking forward to meeting your friends."

"I'm excited you'll finally meet Elsie." I paused. "You know, I've not met any of your friends." It had just occurred to me.

"I don't have a lot," said Jack. He spoke quietly and with finality.

"I expect you don't have a lot of time."

"That, and I'm what you might call selective. I want the best in life and people. That's why I chose you."

Once again, his lips brushed my fingers.

For a few minutes, we drove in silence. I wondered what he would think of Elsie, Alec, and my other friends. Would they meet his standards?

Elsie's book launch took place at Primrose Hill Books in Regent's Park. It felt good to step out of the cold, damp air into the warm shop with its shelves of books and inviting paper smell.

A few rows of folding chairs were at the back of the shop; several seats were occupied. Elsie and Alec were talking with a man with combed-over hair and glasses; he must be the bookseller. When she saw me, her eyes lit up, and she rushed over to us.

"It's lovely to see you, Mandy, thank you so much for coming," she said in her little American voice. When we embraced, she was so petite that I felt as though I were hugging a child.

"I wouldn't miss this for the world, love," I said. "And don't you look gorgeous."

I wasn't exaggerating. Her royal blue dress made her blue eyes appear bluer still, and her face, framed by light brown curls, was as soft and pretty as it had been when she'd met Alec twelve years earlier.

"So do you. And you must be Jack. It's lovely to meet you. Thanks so much for coming."

"My pleasure." Jack smiled kindly as he shook her hand, and I could tell he found her as adorable as I did.

Now Alec was beside Elsie, his arm around her shoulder. I supposed he was good-looking in his way with his high cheekbones and expressive dark eyes. It was funny he and Dave sported the same haircut these days: short with the curved fringe in the center of the forehead. Of course, he wasn't as tall as Dave.

"Hello, Mandy, you all right," he said as he kissed my cheek.

"You all right, Alec. Jack, this is Alec Wilder. Alec, Jack Slayton."

They shook hands, and although they murmured all the right pleasantries, I got a funny feeling in my stomach.

They'd taken an instant dislike to each other.

"Won't you sit down?" said Elsie. "It's almost seven, and we'll be getting started soon."

Jack and I took our seats on two chairs on the end of a row. Thus far, there were six other people present, all of whom seemed to know each other. There was an Indian couple; the woman was very pretty, and she wore a becoming red shawl. Two women—one with short auburn hair, the other with long brown hair—seemed to be together. The last pair was a bearded man and a striking woman with dark hair and pale skin. I recognized her as Lila, Elsie's Egyptologist friend whom I'd consulted when I'd decorated Luxor. I caught her eye and waved.

The shop door opened. "Good to see you, mate," Alec said, and Elsie said something I couldn't hear.

"No way I'd stay away, my dear," said a familiar voice.

I leapt to my feet. Next to me, Jack looked startled.

Stepping over his feet, I made my way to the front of the shop.

A short, slight man with a small, wavy beard and a receding hairline stood by Alec and Elsie. His dark eyes sparkled, and they were laughing at something he had said.

"Lucas!" I cried.

We hugged. "Lovely to see you, Mandy. It's been ages."

Back when he'd been one of Serval's roadies, he'd been my favorite member of the crew. Now he and Alec had their own band, and I was glad he was making a living from music. His girlfriend, Connie, had painted the murals in Luxor, the same ones I'd consulted Lila about.

"Is Connie joining you tonight?"

Elsie winced, and I knew I'd made a blunder.

"No, she left me for her millionaire ex-boyfriend last month," said Lucas ironically. "So I am on my own tonight."

"I'm so sorry—"

"Not a bit of it, my dear. It had run its course, and she's happier without me."

I put an arm around his shoulder. "Come sit by us anyway." I had to make amends somehow.

Jack was standing by the folding chair, staring at us.

"Jack, this is Lucas Sharper. He's Alec's bandmate; in another life, he was part of Serval's crew. Lucas, Jack Slayton."

Jack's eyes were hard as he took Lucas's hand. He did not say it was a pleasure to meet Lucas.

We took our seats so that Lucas was on the inside and Jack on the aisle.

"I know the couple over there," I whispered to Jack. "I'll introduce you after the reading although they'll probably be at the supper since the woman's a good friend of Elsie's."

Jack stared straight ahead as though he couldn't hear me.

"She's the one I consulted about the murals in the salon," I said quietly. "She's an Egyptologist."

I might have been speaking to a mummy. He showed no reaction.

What had bothered him? Lucas had arrived, and suddenly he was angry. I tried to remember what had happened. I had hugged Lucas and then put an arm around his shoulder when I'd learned Connie had left him—surely, Jack didn't think I fancied Lucas. I wanted to laugh.

"I'll just say hello to Lila and Harry," said Lucas.

He bounded up in his quick way, leaving me alone with Jack.

"I've known Lucas for thirteen years," I murmured.

Even with the murmur of conversation around us, Jack's silence was audible.

"He's the brother I never had," I continued. "I invited him to sit with us just now because his girlfriend's just left him."

I paused. "He's the kind you want to mother."

Jack's shoulders relaxed. When he turned to me, his eyes were relieved.

"Then we'll do our best to cheer him up."

There was a bustle behind us. Three women and a thin man with a camera had entered the shop. They consulted with Elsie for a moment before taking their seats in the back row. Then Elsie nodded at the man with the combover and came forward.

As the bookseller introduced Elsie, Jack took my hand. His fingers, laced with mine, felt oddly heavy.

Eighteen

Smiling shyly, Elsie stood before us, a copy of her book in her hands.

"Thank you all for coming tonight," she said. "*The Litter* was born, as many of you know, out of my voluntary work with Cat's Protection. Alec and I have two cats of our own, and we foster cats for our local chapter. My protagonist, Molly, a woman who has struggled with infertility, finds solace and purpose in caring for chronically ill and elderly cats.

She paused. "In this passage, Molly gains the trust of a cat who has been abused."

Then she read the scene in her soft American voice. I could tell it was well-written, even moving, and yet my attention wandered.

My eyes flitted to the other faces in the audience. The bookseller smiled earnestly, his hands folded in his lap. The Indian couple leaned forward in their chairs, the man smiling slightly. The two women who seemed to be together were equally attentive; in fact, tears seemed to form in the eyes of the long-haired one. Lila and her man friend,

Harry, kept their eyes on Elsie, while Lucas's dark eyes registered every syllable.

At the back sat the three women who'd arrived late. Although they looked nothing alike, they all wore the same knowing, Mona Lisa smile. The man who'd come in with them must have been a photographer because he moved discreetly around the room, occasionally snapping photos.

In the front row, Alec gazed at his wife. From where I sat, only his profile was visible. But despite his smile, his eye held an emotion I couldn't quite identify. Pride and wistfulness, I think. Whatever it was, it made me sad.

Jack's fingers pressed my hand, and our eyes met.

Elsie had stopped reading. She smiled at the applause that followed. "Are there any questions?" she asked.

Silence greeted her. She smiled nervously, her fingers tapping the book's cover.

I tried to think of a question, but I drew a blank. Else smiled gratefully when the woman with short hair raised a hand.

"Can you describe your greatest influences?" she asked in a Geordie accent.

Then Lucas inquired about her main character and the Indian woman asked about her writing process. Elsie replied thoughtfully, gaining confidence as she spoke. Finally, one of the women at the back, a slight woman with a pixie cut, asked about her next project.

Elsie laughed self-consciously. "I'm afraid it's rather a departure," she replied. "I've just finished a detective novel. It's set in an English country house, but it takes place in modern times and involves rock musicians. A world I know something about." Once again, she gave a self-deprecating little laugh.

There were no more questions, so Elsie signed copies of her book. Everyone present purchased one, even the bloke taking pictures. While we waited for Elsie to sign our books, we chatted. I introduced Jack to Lila and Harry, and Lila introduced me to the Indian couple, Ravi and Rhada. Then I recalled meeting them years earlier at Elsie and Alec's wedding. When I was introduced to the two women, Clara and Angie, I remembered them, too, a lesbian couple who'd also attended the wedding. Clara, the short-haired one, was a lecturer somewhere up north, while her friend was the matron of a pediatric ward in the same city.

Then it was my turn to have Elsie sign my book. Her eyes moist, she sat at her table and smiled up at me.

"That was brilliant, love," I said. "You're a lovely writer."

I felt a bit guilty saying that as my attention had wandered during the reading, but I'd read her book, and I meant every word of it.

She wrote quickly and handed it back to me, smiling shyly.

Her inscription put a lump in my throat:

Dear Mandy,

Thank you for your friendship and support over the years, especially for reading my little book.

Love always, Elsie

Then she signed Jack's book and Lucas's, and then there were no more books to sign. Nodding to Alec, she rose from her chair.

"I guess we're going to supper," she said wryly. "You're all invited, of course."

The bookseller shook his head when she urged him to come. "I'd love to, but I have to close the shop."

Rising from her chair, Elsie looked drained. She'd been cheerful enough during the event; I hoped the small turnout wouldn't upset her too much.

The trio of women who'd entered together hovered near the shop's door. The tallest, a full-figured brunette with a bob, rolled a cigarette. At Elsie's approach, she smiled warmly.

"I'm sorry," said Elsie.

"For what, my dear?" Her voice was silky, yet husky; it was easy to imagine her as a jazz singer.

"For being a flop."

"Now, there's no need to talk like that. *The Litter* had a successful launch."

"With fifteen people in the audience? Ten if you deduct my editors, the photographer, and the bookseller. And those ten wouldn't be there if they weren't my friends."

"Now, chin up, Elsie. It's quality, not quantity. It's not how many, but who."

She exchanged knowing smiles with the other two women, and I had the impression they were three good witches.

"You're kind. Are you coming to supper?"

"We'd love to, but we've got a few things to sort out. Good night, my dear."

She patted Elsie on the head as though Elsie were a little girl. The other two women smiled indulgently, and they left in a plume of her spicy perfume.

"Who was that?" I asked.

"My editor, Christine. She happens to be friends with the other two. Helena, the one with long dark hair, writes for the *Guardian's* Books page, and Suzanne, the one with short hair, is my editor at *Hearth and Home.*"

I smiled. "Then I should feel very good about the launch, love. She sounded very confident."

Elsie grimaced. "I think they were just being nice."

Alec had booked a private room at Odette's a few doors down. The group from the bookseller walked over, Jack's arm around my shoulder. Ravi and Rhada were just ahead of us, and Ravi made a show of handing Rhada over little puddles on the pavement. Then Jack, laughing, extended his hand gallantly to me. He was more lighthearted than usual, and it was pleasant to see this side of him.

Once we were at the restaurant, we settled around a long table in the private room. A waiter brought two bottles of champagne. Once our glasses were poured, Alec rose to his feet and raised his glass.

"To my Elsie," he said in his northern voice. "And her brilliant book. I couldn't be prouder."

Lila glanced at Alec. Although she drank with the rest of us, her grey eyes were cool.

I wondered why she would dislike Alec. Then I remembered one of the last arguments I'd had with Dave before our divorce. We were supposed to go to Alec and Elsie's for the weekend, and as we got ready, we had a row in the bedroom.

"Next thing you'll be telling me Alec cheated on Elsie," I'd snapped.

Dave sighed. Eyes downcast, he muttered, "He loves her, Mandy, he really does."

"What's that supposed to mean?" I exclaimed. Suddenly, my own hurts were forgotten.

"Well, Elsie wasn't herself for a bit, and Alec was drinking more during that time." He paused. "He thinks the world of her, Mandy."

We'd decided against going away that weekend.

Lila was one of Elsie's closest friends. No wonder she distrusted Alec. Given my own history, I couldn't blame her. But obviously Alec and Elsie had worked it out, unlike Dave and me.

Jack and I sat opposite Rhada and Ravi. Over steak, Jack learned that Ravi was a barrister whose practice consisted mainly of criminal defense.

Jack frowned. "I should have thought there was more money in prosecution or insurance, that sort of thing."

Ravi smiled. "Money, yes. But not the interest. I enjoy a challenge, and the defense is never short of that."

"I shouldn't have thought defense was all that challenging for you," said Elsie. "You were always defending Lila and me from Mrs. Barrymore in the old days."

Again, Ravi grinned. "Mrs. Barrymore would have made a most able prosecutor or even a judge."

"Mrs. Barrymore was their landlady when they were all at university in Manchester," I said to Jack. "She was a bit of a dragon, and Elsie knew she'd disapprove of Alec being a rock musician, so Ravi told her he was a classical violinist. She believed him—until she saw Serval on *Top of the Pops*."

Jack chuckled. "All the same, though, you might broaden your scope a bit. After all, what's the use in keeping some lowlife out of prison when you might earn real money?"

Ravi studied his fork and knife. "I should think it means a great deal to the lowlife in question."

As the meal progressed, Jack spoke with Alec, who sat beside him.

"Mandy tells me you have your own band," said Jack.

"Yes, Lucas and I tour as Nest Egg. We play bluesy rock."

"How much of a market is there for that sort of thing?"

"We've got a decent fanbase, nothing like Serval days. But we're playing music we like, and it's a living."

Over his glass, Jack peered at Alec. "I don't know much about the music business, but I suppose there are ways to increase revenue? Ticket and record sales and such?"

Alec's fork froze in midair, and his mouth tightened.

My stomach turned. Jack meant well, bless him, but I wished he wouldn't give business advice to people he'd just met on a night out.

Alec set down his fork. "There are," he said evenly. "And someday, Lucas and I will explore them. Probably not tonight, though."

Then Alec turned to Clara, and that was the end of that conversation. I could have sighed with relief, but took a mouthful of chardonnay instead.

Only Elsie, Lila, and Rhada ordered dessert. As we waited for it to arrive, Lucas smiled at Elsie from the other end of the table.

"And I hope we'll meet again this time next year, Elsa, my dear," he said. "To celebrate your next book."

Elsie twisted her dangling pearl earrings. "I don't know," she said ruefully. "My first book's not going to be a success. After one dismal performance, I'm not sure the publisher will go through with the second."

Jack turned to Elsie, who sat on the other side of Alec. "I don't know much about publishing," he began, "but I expect you're doing something about publicity."

Elsie's eyes were large as she twisted a stray curl around her finger. "I suppose so. There was the reading, of course. There may be others. There may be something in the *Guardian*. And my magazine may run something."

Jack nodded. "Excellent. Now here's a question: why do you write under Elsa Farrell and not Elsa Wilder?"

Now real alarm filled Elsie's blue eyes. "I—I don't know. Yes, well, when I started writing my column, I didn't want people to think of me as a rock musician's wife who wrote. That's not what I wanted it to be about, and it's not how I wanted readers to see me. I wanted to write about being an American married to an Englishman, an ordinary Kent housewife. So I used my maiden name, it became my professional name, and it made sense to continue using it when I published my novel."

Jack's eyes were keen. "And is that what you want your writing career to be? An extension of your column for a women's monthly?"

I placed a hand on Jack's arm, but I was too late. Elsie looked small and deflated; the damage had been done.

"I don't know. I write what I want to write, I suppose."

"And it sounds as though you've written two utterly different books. I mean, you wouldn't find them on the same shelf at the bookseller."

"No."

Alec's face had gone very pale. If we'd been in an ordinary pub up North, he would have punched Jack by now.

Once again, I touched Jack's arm, but he seemed not to notice.

"Again, I don't know much about the literary world, but it seems to me you'd fare better if you became known for one kind of book. So readers would know what they were getting. And you shouldn't be afraid to use your husband's name—it might make more people pick up your book."

Staring at her empty plate, Elsie looked smaller than ever.

"I know I've written a little book," she said finally. "It's never going to be a bestseller, and it won't make the Booker longlist either. The most I can hope for is that a few people enjoy it."

"I loved it!" I cried.

"Quite a few people already love it," said Angie quietly. "And every word of it is true."

Something about her tone made me look at her. It hadn't occurred to me that lesbians could want children, but obviously she did, poor girl.

"And you enjoyed writing it," said Lucas firmly. "You write what you want to write—that's what makes you a serious writer."

"And when it comes to readership, pet, you've already got most of us beat," said Clara. "I write for respected scholarly journals—and they don't have an eighth of the readership of your column."

"I think the most I've gotten is a couple hundred readers," said Lila. "And that was an article I wrote about pyramids for a children's magazine. Assuming all the children who had the magazine actually read it, that is."

Rhada laughed. "And the literary magazine that publishes my poems has perhaps a few dozen subscribers. Elsie is the successful writer here."

Alec cleared his throat and turned to Jack.

"The thing about my wife, mate," he said, "is that she doesn't need me to prop her up or boost her reputation. In fact, she would have gone farther and accomplished more without me. I love her, and I'm proud of her, but that's the truth."

Now Elsie's blue eyes were moist. She exchanged a look with Alec, and apart from her wedding day, I had never seen her look prettier.

Ravi stood and raised his glass. "To Elsie's literary career," he said. "May she enjoy many more triumphs."

"Here, here," echoed Harry, and once again, we raised our glasses.

After dessert, Jack offered cigars to the men.

Ravi flashed white teeth. "Thank you, but I do not smoke."

Harry and Lucas also declined, declaring they'd smoked enough fags that night.

Smiling then, Jack turned to Alec, a cigar outstretched. "Have a smoke?"

Alec's intake of breath was slight, but I heard it.

"No thanks, mate," he said. "Not tonight."

Jack blinked. They were good cigars, imported from Cuba, and it had never occurred to him that all the men would decline them. I couldn't help feeling sorry for him.

Then his eyes alighted on Clara. "Would you like a cigar?" he asked, smiling.

Lila gulped back something that might have been a laugh.

Clara crushed the cigarette she'd been smoking. "No, thanks. I'm surprised matron here still allows me the occasional fag on a festive evening."

"Not for long," said Angie with a smile, and the conversation turned to other things.

Jack smoked his cigar as I finished my wine. I was surprised that he'd lit it when no one else had accepted one. He probably felt he'd earned it.

The mood was lighter then, and when the dinner ended, we exchanged hugs and handshakes with the others.

"Ring me, love," I whispered when I embraced Elsie.

Alec managed to shake Jack's hand quite civilly. Jack and I held hands as we followed him and Elsie into the night.

Alec had booked a room at a hotel nearby. As they rounded a corner, he scooped Elsie into his arms, and she laughed. No one who saw them would have guessed that they had been married for nearly twelve years, let alone that they'd had their share of troubles in that time.

At that moment, I envied Elsie. She was spending the night in the arms of someone who loved her.

Then I realized I was, too.

Nineteen

J ack and I spent Friday and Saturday night at my house. On Sunday morning, he kissed my neck as I lay in his arms.

"See if your ex-husband can keep the kids for a couple more nights," he murmured.

"They have school, remember." He needed a shave, and his stubble felt nice on my neck.

"And presumably he can drive them there or put them on a bus."

"Yes, as long as he doesn't have work that day." I paused. "Of course, he's not had much lately."

"Good." Now his mouth was on the nape of my neck.

"Just what are you planning?"

He continued to kiss me. "There's a property in Bath I think you'll like. I thought we might drive there on Monday and take a look."

I sat up. "So it's business. And here I was thinking you wanted another lazy morning in bed."

The lines around Jack's eyes crinkled. "That, too."

When I rang Dave that afternoon, he cheerfully agreed to keep the kids another two nights.

"Happy to do it," he said. "And it's no problem at all, carrying them to and from school. I'll bring them round to Mrs. Jones's on Tuesday after school."

"You're sure it won't interfere with your work—"

Dave snorted. "Work! I've got a short gig Monday whilst they're at school. Nothing at all on Tuesday. That's the joy of being a session musician these days. You don't earn enough to support a family, but you've got all the time in the world to take the kids to the park." He laughed bitterly.

I couldn't help but cringe for him. "Dave, I'm sorry—"

"Don't be. It'll be good to have a couple more days with Katie and Sam. And I'm happy to help you, Mandy. Really. I can always mind them if you need to go out."

"Thanks, Dave."

"And I'm proud—happy your salon is doing so well. You're obviously doing something right."

"Thanks, Dave, that's lovely." It was, too, but I couldn't think of anything else to say.

The silence on the phone became loud.

"Well, thanks again," I said. "I guess I'll see you in a couple weeks. When it's your turn again."

"Yes," replied Dave quietly. "Bye, Mandy."

***

Like most salons, Luxor was closed on Mondays, so Jack and I were able to have a nice lie-in before we left for Bath.

"It's luxurious!" he said, one arm around my bare shoulder.

"Look at you punning!" But he was sweet in these lighthearted moods.

We sped down the M4, easily arriving in time to meet the estate agent. It was a clear, cold day, and the sandstone buildings looked golden in the sunlight. I'd always loved Bath with its graceful Georgian buildings and posh boutiques. As I walked along York Street, my hand in Jack's, I thought how nice it would be to have an excuse to come there regularly. Of course, my Chelsea salon would come first, but I'd have to pop to Bath to check on the staff there. And whilst I was there, I could do a bit of shopping and have lunch.

"It'd be lovely to come here more often," I said.

Jack squeezed my hand.

The estate agent was young, in his twenties, with wavy blond hair combed back from his forehead. He met us at the property, a large storefront just off North Parade Passage. He shook hands with us pleasantly enough, but he jangled his keys in his pockets as we inspected the premises.

His impatience ought to have annoyed me, but it didn't. I couldn't help but be struck by the way the light entered the front window. Even on a winter day, it was bright. And although the walls were pink, it was easy to envision them painted gold and adorned with more Egyptian paintings. Perhaps Lucas's ex-girlfriend would be up for another commission. And since it had been a salon, there would be no need to install mirrors or sinks.

Jack's eyes met mine in a mirror.

"Well, what do you think, Mandy?" he asked.

The look I flashed him was all the answer he needed. His blue eyes were triumphant as he returned my smile.

The estate agent stopped jangling his keys. "Yes, is there any interest?"

Jack's eyes met mine. He was leaving it up to me.

"Yes," I said, for this time I couldn't think of a reason to say no.

Twenty

On Tuesday morning, Robbie, Rose, and Betty were at the front desk when I arrived at Luxor.

Robbie lifted one eyebrow. "How was the dirty weekend, then, Mandy darlin'?"

I set my bag on the desk. "Not very dirty. Though it was longer than we planned. Dave agreed to keep the kids on Sunday and Monday so that we could go to Bath."

"To do a bit of shopping," suggested Rose.

"To look at another salon, actually."

By now, Robbie had returned his attention to the salon's diary. "And it was too big or too small, was it, or maybe the light wasn't quite right."

He thought he was so clever, that one.

I held my head a little higher. "It was perfect, actually. As a matter of fact, we're buying it."

At that, Robbie jerked his head up. Now his green eyes were large, and I could feel Betty's and Rose's eyes on me. My lips formed what must have been a smirk. None of them had believed there really would be a Luxor II.

"That's brilliant, love," said Betty. "Is Jack buying the place with you, then?"

"He's putting up most of the capital. But the business will be in my name."

"But we'll still see you? After you open your other salon?" Real worry lurked in Rose's dark eyes.

"Of course!" I exclaimed. "This salon and our clients and all of you will still be my main focus."

All three of them were still gazing at me expectantly, so I felt I ought to say something else.

"Anyway," I continued cheerfully, "it will be another month or more before it's all settled. The lawyers and the estate agents and Jack have their bits to do before we settle. And then it will take a few months to get the salon up and running. For the time being, I'm very much here."

They returned my smile nervously, but since their shoulders relaxed a bit, I supposed the news reassured them. For some reason, it reassured me, too.

***

It was a busy day, so I didn't have much time to think about Luxor II. Since my morning appointments ran late, I barely had time to down a salad for lunch. As I munched my lettuce, I wondered if it wasn't a blessing, this not having time to think.

In the midafternoon, there was finally a lull. "I see Elsie's book launch was a success," remarked Betty when we stood at the desk.

I wrinkled my nose. "It was lovely, but I wouldn't say that. There were only fifteen people, including her and the bookseller. But she put a good face on it, bless her."

Now it was Betty's turn to raise an eyebrow. "That's not what I gathered from the *Guardian*."

"What?"

"I brought a copy of Saturday's *Guardian* for you to read." She rummaged in her bag. "Here it is. I meant to show you first thing, but we were busy."

The newspaper she handed me was turned to the Books section. Elsie's launch had made the front page. There was a photo of her holding her book and looking radiant in her dress. But it wasn't the only picture accompanying the article.

In one photo, Lila and Clara appeared deep in conversation. "Dr. Lila Hedges of the University of Bristol discusses the novel with Dr. Clara Brown of Newcastle University," read the caption.

Then, there was a shot of Alec and Lucas laughing. "Nest Egg guitarist Alec Wilder has a laugh with Lucas Sharper, the band's bassist and vocalist," the caption proclaimed.

Finally, there was a photo of Jack and me chatting with Ravi and Rhada. "Property developer Jack Slayton and Luxor salon owner Mandy Wilt catch up with Mr. Ravi Singh, barrister, and Mrs. Rhada Singh," announced the *Guardian*.

Put that way, we sounded rather important.

I read the first paragraph:

> "What do an Egyptologist, a scholar in the late Victorian novel, a barrister, a property developer, a blues rock duo, and the proprietor of Chelsea's trendiest salon have in common? They all attended the launch

of Elsa Farrell's debut novel, *The Litter*, on Thursday night at Primrose Hill Books."

I skimmed the article. Although the writer said some nice things about the book and Elsie's writing, she focused on the mystery of Elsa Farrell, a debut novelist and women's monthly columnist, who had a devoted and glittering following.

"You know, I had a feeling Elsie's editors had something in mind," I said, handing the paper back to Betty. "They seemed so confident even though only a few people came. Good for Elsie. I'll ring her tonight."

"Oh, people will be beating down the doors to get her book now," said Betty. "I'm glad for Elsie. I'll have to get over to Waterstones to get a copy for myself."

The door swung open, letting a rush of cold air into the salon. I glanced up from the diary to see Dave standing in the doorway wearing a light denim jacket.

"You're supposed to be looking after the kids!" I cried. It was like to him to forget what he was supposed to be doing and show up out of nowhere.

Dave toyed with the end of his mustache. "And I've brought one with me," he said ironically.

And sure enough, there was Katie peeping behind her father in her little plaid uniform.

"Hello, sweetie," I said, stepping forward and folding her in my arms.

Then I turned sharply to Dave. "Where's Sam?"

"Round his mate Gareth's house. Gareth's mum said she'd give him a lift home." He paused. "I thought I'd bring Katie here rather than send her on the bus alone."

I bit my lip. Here I'd been screeching at him like a shrew, and all the while he'd been a responsible dad.

"Hello, Betty," said Dave, for Betty was standing next to me.

"You all right, Dave." She smiled down at Katie. "I'm Betty. I don't suppose you remember me, but I remember you when you were a baby."

"Hello, Betty," said Katie politely.

"Do you like peppermints? I've got some at the desk."

Katie nodded, and they walked to the desk. Not for the first time, I was grateful for Betty's tact.

Now we were alone. I smiled sheepishly at Dave.

"I'm sorry. I'd no right to greet you like that, especially when you'd kept the kids an extra two days."

Again, Dave twisted an end of his mustache with one finger. "Well, I did turn up like a bad penny. I've got a bad habit of doing that. And I brought only one kiddie. You had a right to be suspicious. In your shoes, I should have called the police."

His eyes laughed, so I did, too.

"Anyway, thanks for looking after Katie and Sam."

"No worries." He stuck his hands in his pockets. "How was Bath?"

"Brilliant. In fact, we're going through with it."

"You're buying the salon? Mandy, that's fantastic!"

He was so genuinely pleased for me, it was hard to believe he was the same man who'd often told me, only half-jokingly, that women were for doing the washing up and looking after the kiddies.

"Thanks."

"So when will you move in, then? To the other salon?"

"It'll be at least a month, maybe more. Jack and the lawyers and the estate agents have to work it all out. Jack knows more about it than I do."

His eyes darted to my face and then down to the floor. "Joint venture, is it?"

"He's putting up most of the capital. But it'll be in my name."

He nodded as if to show he understood. Then for a moment, we stood there, smiling at each other, not knowing what to say.

Dave coughed. "I've some good news of my own."

"What is it?"

"Today, whilst the kids were at school, I went up to a shop on Denmark Street to look at some drumsticks. I know the proprietor well. We got to chatting, and apparently, he's got a vacancy on the shop floor. He needs someone with a background in percussion." He paused. "I start Monday next."

"Full time?"

Dave gave a quick nod. "Five days a week and the odd Saturday."

"Dave, that's brilliant!" I exclaimed.

He was standing taller and holding his head higher than he had in a long time—since Serval broke up at any rate. He certainly looked more confident than he had when he wandered into Luxor that day in November.

Then a thought crossed my mind, and I wrinkled my forehead.

"But, Dave—what about your drumming?"

He chuckled. "I'll be surrounded by drums all the time, Mandy. I won't be able to get away."

"I mean, your career. Your work as a musician."

"I could barely keep the wolves from the door. Couldn't, really. There's no living in session work these days."

"But you've got to play," I spluttered. "You've got so much talent."

The idea of Dave not drumming made me sad. Without knowing what I was doing, I stepped forward and placed a hand on his upper arm.

Dave stared at me, his blue eyes moist.

"I've not given up music, Mandy," he said gently. "I still play in a pub band. I'm not John Bonham, but I can manage the intro to "Ballroom Blitz" or "Radar Love" on a Thursday night." He laughed.

"And even if I gave that up," he continued, "it's a small price to pay for a week's wages and being able to say I'm going to work every day."

My hand was still on his arm. I pulled it back.

"Glad you're still drumming," I muttered.

Now Dave was studying me closely.

"Listen, Mandy," he said. "Katie's in good hands with Betty. If you're able to grab a drink—"

I rose to my full height. "No, thanks. I've got a client coming in a few minutes. In fact, there she is now. But congratulations on your job. Hello, Minty!"

I greeted Minty Paige with more enthusiasm than I felt and left Dave to say goodbye to Katie and Betty.

After Minty had her usual cut, I gave Katie a tour of the salon. She'd never been to Luxor before, so it was fun to show her my work. She was fascinated by little things like the wardrobe where we kept the towels and the chemicals we used to clean combs and shears.

But the Egyptian murals interested her most of all. She had ques tions about them I couldn't answer, like the names of the various gods and goddesses. I did the best I could.

"I'll have to write to Aunt Elsie's friend Lila," I said. "She's an Egyptologist so she knows all about these things."

Katie nodded solemnly. Then she pointed to the mural in front of us, which showed a line of pharaohs in their big headdresses.

"That one looks like Jack, Mummy."

I laughed. "I see what you mean."

Now that she pointed it out, that pharaoh did have a look of Jack. There was something steely about his mouth, a quiet confidence in the way he occupied his throne.

"And that one looks like Daddy."

My eyes followed her finger. The pharaoh in question was tall and lanky, and even in his headdress, there was something relaxed about him, a wry smile lurking on his lips. Give him blue eyes and a mustache, and he'd be Dave in fancy dress.

"So he does."

Now Katie turned to look up at me. Beneath her blonde ponytails, her blue eyes regarded me steadily.

"Which one do you like better, Mummy?"

I inhaled sharply.

"That's quite enough out of you," I said. "Now you go and talk to Betty."

She trotted off to the front desk where, no doubt, another peppermint or perhaps a biscuit awaited her.

I shook my head as I prepared for the day's last client. She was all too knowing, that one, and I'd gone soft, letting her get away with that cheek. My mum would have boxed my ears.

Twenty-One

In early March, Katie had her first piano recital. Of course, it was too much to expect my family to come to London for the occasion.

Mum, bless her, couldn't tear herself away from the bed and breakfast. "I simply couldn't leave Mark on his own in Torquay," she said. "You know what Devon's like that time of year."

I didn't know there was a rush of holidaymakers in the West Country in March. But she probably couldn't leave Mark alone with a full bar, and anyway, it was a long drive or train journey from Torquay to London.

And Kate, of course, couldn't tear herself away from the tennis court or the neighbors' cocktail party.

But Jack seemed genuinely delighted when I invited him one Sunday afternoon when we were side by side on the loveseat in my front room.

"Of course, Mandy," he declared. "We need to support Katie."

My face flushed with pleasure. He cared enough about Katie and me to sit through an afternoon of little girls playing the piano in a church.

"You're lovely, you know that," I said.

Little lines formed around his blue eyes as they narrowed and softened. "I might say the same about you," he said, putting an arm around my shoulder.

At moments like these, it was hard to remember he was the same Jack who gave me business advice.

I laughed. "At least Katie's musical, so it shouldn't be too painful to sit through her performance. She takes after her dad. So does Sam, being so good at sport. Good thing they both got his talent."

"I wouldn't say that." All of a sudden, Jack was serious. "I hope they've inherited your brains and initiative. You'll want them to make something of themselves, and talent's nothing without hard work and common sense."

I sat up straight. "Dave worked hard to get where he did with Serval," I said sharply. "He's working hard now; it's just that the band broke up and the music world's changed. There's not the same need for drummers that there was a few years ago."

"We've all got to adapt to the times—"

"He has adapted," I snapped. "He's working in a shop in Denmark Street."

"It's just that I don't like to see you taken advantage of—"

"He always pays his maintenance. Always has even when he was on the dole."

Jack opened his mouth and then closed it as though he thought better of what he was about to say.

He smiled. "Well, enough about him. I'm more interested in you. And Katie and Sam, of course. And speaking of initiative, things are moving forward with Luxor II."

"Oh?"

I fingered the afghan on the loveseat's arm. Whenever he talked about solicitors and estate agents, my mind wandered. I wanted to show interest—he was doing this for me after all—but it was like when I had boring teachers at school. I found myself looking out the window or thinking about something I'd seen on telly or wondering what I wanted for tea.

"Yes, we'll get a better deal than we reckoned. Several thousand less."

"Fabulous!" I said and meant it. "So what would you like for dinner?"

***

The Friday before the recital was a busy one at Luxor. Nancy Phillips, one of my favorite clients, was on the schedule, and I looked forward to talking to her.

I was quite surprised when I came out front to greet her and found Jack sitting beside her. He stood up when he saw me.

"Jack, what a surprise!" I exclaimed.

"Hello, Mandy," he said, taking my hand. "Sorry to bother you at work."

"It's not a bother—"

"It's just that something's come up with one of my properties in Glasgow. I'll need to see to it this weekend, so I won't be able to make Katie's recital. Please give her my apologies—and I'm sorry, Mandy."

I could tell he felt bad. "It's all right," I said. "You do what you have to do."

"I'll call you when I'm back in the smoke."

He kissed me and then pressed my hand before striding from the salon.

I greeted Nancy and invited her back to my chair.

"Is that your boyfriend?" she asked. Then she laughed. "Of course, he is, what a silly question. Anyway, he's lovely."

"I think so."

"He's so kind." She laughed a bit self-consciously as she sat before the sink. "When he came in, Betty told him you would be out in a few minutes. He sat beside me, and I said I was your client. He asked me what I did for a living, and of course, I said I'd been a secretary at Randell and McCartney for eight years. But somehow, I found myself telling him I had a degree in English and still wanted to be a copywriter."

My fingers worked the shampoo through the warm water and her short, fine fair hair. It didn't surprise me that she'd opened up to Jack. He could intimidate people when he wanted to, but he was gentle with the children.

"He told me there was no reason I couldn't be a copywriter even after all those years of typing and answering phones and making tea. He told me exactly what to say to the chief of copy."

Her eyes were huge as she raised them to me. "Mandy—should I believe him?"

I laughed. "I should think so. Jack's a very successful property developer, and he's made his money all on his own. And he likes taking people under his wing and helping them grow. If he didn't think you were capable of being a copywriter, he wouldn't have bothered."

"Thank you, Mandy!" Her eyes were very bright.

"You're very welcome, love."

As I rinsed her hair, I reflected how lucky I was to have someone like Jack in my life. He wanted others to make the most of themselves just as he had. He'd been a bit dense at Elsie's book launch, bless him, but he meant well. And it would be good to see Nancy at least try her hand at writing some copy.

And Jack wanted me to be the best salon owner I could be. I hoped I could meet his expectations.

***

The recital took place in a church in a borough west of Ealing. I parked the Cavalier in the small car park, and then Katie, Sam, and I filed into church with the other parents and children.

In the church's narthex, I smiled down at Katie and squeezed her hand. She looked so pretty in her light blue sailor dress and matching Alice band.

"Now, there's nothing to be nervous about," I said. "You'll be brilliant, sweetie. Think of how much you practiced."

Her blue eyes gazed curiously at me. "Why would I be nervous, Mummy?"

"Well, people are often nervous before they go on stage. Actors and such. Sometimes, Daddy used to get nervous before gigs and concerts."

I didn't add that he often took Dutch courage with a shot or two.

She studied me, and I found myself feeling oddly self-conscious under her scrutiny.

"Why don't you go sit by Mrs. Tillman?" I asked.

She nodded solemnly and walked to the front of the church. There, Mrs. Tillman, a slightly stooped lady with a grey permanent, was arranging children in the first few pews.

"She's a strange one," Sam declared.

"She's confident," I said brightly. "I think it's wonderful."

"She's a strange one," he repeated, and part of me agreed with him.

We sat near the front of the church. Around us was the murmur of voices and the rustle of coats as other families settled themselves in the pews.

Discreetly, I scanned the room. I didn't know any of the other parents, but I wondered if Dave had arrived. I hadn't seen his black Golf in the car park, but he might have parked up the street.

No Dave. I hoped he would come. Music was something he and Katie had in common, and funny though she was, I knew she would be gutted if he didn't attend.

But Mrs. Tillman was moving to the front of the church. She stood in front of the altar rail and smiled kindly at us. With her grey cardigan and grey permanent, she looked very much at home in the church. It occurred to me that people like Mrs. Tillman were the reason children could take piano lessons or attend Sunday school, not that mine ever went to church. Every village or borough needed a Mrs. Tillman, and I hoped there would always be Mrs. Tillmans.

"Good afternoon, ladies and gentlemen," she began. "Welcome to St. Cecilia's Parish Church. St. Cecilia is the patron saint of musicians, so it's fitting that our afternoon of music is taking place here—"

Behind me, a door squeaked open. I turned to see Dave's lanky frame step over the threshold. With his old brown sport coat and downcast eyes, he looked like a dog who knew he'd done wrong; even his mustache drooped more than usual. I instantly forgave him for being late.

But instead of coming into the church, he lingered in the entryway. He was holding the door for someone: a blonde girl. Probably one of Mrs. Tillman's older pupils.

I returned my gaze to Mrs. Tillman.

"We have a lovely selection of music for you this afternoon," she was saying. "I do hope you enjoy it." She was a perfect poppet.

I wondered where Dave was sitting. My eyes scanned the back of the church. He'd found a seat in the second pew from the back. He was removing his sport coat and whispering to someone. The blonde girl who'd entered when he did. In fact, she was sitting beside him.

She'd come in with him.

She wasn't one of Mrs. Tillman's pupils.

She was his girlfriend.

Twenty-Two

The girl must have felt my gaze for she glanced in my direction. Our eyes met. Hers were curious and a bit timid.

She knew I was Dave's ex-wife all right.

Sharply, I faced the front of the church. I wouldn't let Dave or this girl or anyone ruin Katie's recital. I made myself listen to a girl a little older than Katie plod her way through a piece.

Dave had never mentioned a girlfriend. Oh, I knew there'd been a few in the first couple years after the divorce though they'd never lasted long and he'd never introduced them to the kids. In fact, I only knew they existed because I'd fished a bit with Elsie and Alec. They'd never have told me voluntarily.

And what did the girl want with Dave? He was still good looking in his lazy way, but he was thirty-eight, and she didn't look much over sixteen. He hadn't been rich for years, and she was probably too young to remember Serval at the height of their fame. Apart from devout Serval fans, few people would even recognize him as a once famous musician.

Between performances, I cast a few discreet looks in their direction. The more I looked at the girl, the younger she looked. She was very slight, her blonde hair was pulled back into a ponytail, and she didn't seem to be wearing any makeup. In fact, there was a shyness about her. She didn't seem like the type to throw herself at a musician old enough to be her father or anyone for that matter.

Surely, Dave wasn't taking advantage of an innocent teenager. He'd lived the life of a rock 'n' roller when Serval was together—that was why we'd gotten divorced, after all—and eventually, his cheating had followed him home, but I didn't think he would do that.

I tossed these thoughts over and over, but I managed to silence them when Katie walked to the piano. She approached the instrument almost solemnly and sat down. For a moment, she hesitated. I held my breath. Was she going to succumb to stage fright even after all her bravado?

But her fingers touched the keys, and she launched into her Mozart minuet. She seemed utterly absorbed in the music the way orchestra musicians always looked on the telly. She played it flawlessly and then stood up to take her bow.

Around us, the applause was loud. Even Sam and the other pupils' parents were grinning; she looked so serious and adorable.

I was so proud of her. Funny to think that Dave and I had produced a little concert pianist. I turned to exchange glances with him.

He was standing and applauding, a big grin on his face. Beside him, also on her feet, was the blonde girl.

In my excitement about Katie, I'd forgotten about her. I turned quickly before my eyes could meet his.

After the recital, there was a reception for pupils and parents at the church hall. Dave and his girlfriend, I was relieved to see, didn't linger after the performance; they just said their goodbyes to Katie and Sam.

I stood at a distance. I wasn't pleased when I saw Dave and then the girl embrace the children. To my surprise, Katie returned her hug.

Katie didn't hug strangers. That meant she'd met the girl before.

I didn't mention Dave or the girl at the reception. I thanked Mrs. Tillman for her efforts with Katie and complimented her on the recital. I ate too many biscuits and told the little girl sitting near us how beautifully she'd played.

Neither Katie nor Sam seemed surprised that Dave had brought his girlfriend to the recital. I decided to ask them about her casually.

"Well, that was lovely," I said cheerfully once we were headed back to Ealing in the Cavalier. "I'm so glad your dad was able to come."

I paused. "Had you met his friend before?"

In the rearview mirror, Katie nodded. "She's Chrissy."

"She stayed at Dad's last weekend," added Sam. "That's where we saw her last."

Strange they hadn't mentioned it when I'd asked them about their weekend with their dad. Then again, perhaps they had—and I hadn't heard. I'd been distracted of late with plans for Luxor II. I felt a pang of guilt.

"She stayed in my room," said Katie. "She said it was like a slumber party, and she wished we could see each other more often."

My eyebrows drew together. I didn't know whether to laugh or cry. Dave was dating a teenager, he'd introduced her to our children, and the girl wanted to befriend Katie.

"We'll see about that," I said as lightly as I could.

Twenty-Three

I tried very hard not to think about Dave and Chrissy that week. And fortunately, between the salon and the kids and the plans for Luxor II, I didn't have much time for them during the day.

But there were the nights. After the kids went to bed, I'd lie awake, staring at the ceiling. Over and over, I'd replay the scenes from the recital. Dave entering the church with the girl at his heels. The two of them seated side by side in the pew. The girl's large eyes staring timidly at me. Katie and Sam speaking nonchalantly of her on the ride home.

Poor kids. They not only had a father who'd taken up with a teenager; they had a mother who was too distracted to listen to them when they'd told her about Dad's new bird.

But a teenager! Surely, Dave wouldn't take advantage of an under-age girl. And even if the girl were a bit older than she looked—let's say nineteen—what would such a young girl want with a man in his late thirties? Especially one who was barely scraping by with a job at a shop, even if it was one of the best places to buy instruments in London. A guy with two kids and an ever-ailing Volkswagen Golf and a little flat in Shepherd's Bush.

But even as I asked myself the question, I knew the answer.

With his tall, lanky frame and lazy smile, Dave was still attractive. And some girls liked older blokes. And his stories about his career would appeal to a girl who liked music or maybe just musicians.

He'd met enough of them on the road.

Once, I'd believed Dave was different to Greg and Billy, Serval's singer and bassist. I knew they'd sleep with anything female when they were on tour. And because Dave alluded to their escapades, I trusted him and pitied their wives.

It was Elsie who'd sowed the first seed of doubt—all by accident, of course. We both married in 1973, and in early 1974, we met for tea in London. I'd taken her to tea at Harrods the first time we'd met in London, and I thought it might be fun to have tea there again—this time in the Georgian, wearing hats and surrounded by a bunch of older ladies who would have been horrified if they knew they were eating their sandwiches and sipping their tea next to rock musicians' wives.

I could remember the moment as if it were yesterday. Between bites of Victoria sponge, I said I felt sorry for Betty and Irene with the band going on tour, knowing what their husbands were like.

A very strange look came over Elsie's face. She stared at her cake as though she couldn't face another bite.

But it only lasted a few seconds.

"I'm thinking of doing some decorating whilst Alec's away," she said brightly. "We've got spare bedrooms, but he's not done anything with them if you know what I mean."

Then we prattled on about decorating. We were two young wives with plenty of money, so it was something we had in common.

But I felt the uncertainty beneath the chatter. Later, I recognized it as the moment I realized Elsie knew something I didn't.

For a couple years, I told myself Dave—and Alec—weren't like the others. It was easy to do. Dave was affectionate when we were together, and he was generous to my family. It was he who'd suggested we pay Kate's fees at the secretarial college; he would have put her through university if that was what she wanted.

And Dave was a doting father. He couldn't spend enough time with the kids when he was at home. He read to them and sang to them, and despite everything he said about women's work, he changed his share of nappies. As soon as Sam could walk, he had him kicking a football in the back garden. When he called home, he insisted on speaking to both of them to tell them he loved them.

Come to think of it, he called me every night—or day—for the first couple years of our marriage. Sometimes, we had proper chats, but often he just rang to tell me he loved and missed me.

Then the calls became less frequent. He always said he loved me, but he usually rang during the day, and our conversations were hurried. Then he'd skip a day or two, and when he called again, he'd apologize, saying he'd been too tired to call the day before or that Alec had made him practice a passage or have another pint.

I wanted to believe him, so I did. And when he was at home, he was as affectionate as ever.

Then, he started getting calls at home. He'd always tell me it was his sister, Maureen, or Gladys, the band's secretary. But he always needed privacy for these conversations. Not that they lasted very long.

One day, I passed the lounge whilst he was on the phone. "I told you not to call me at home," he said.

It was a strange thing to tell his sister or, for that matter, the band's secretary. I trusted Gladys, who wore bottle glasses and loved her fiancé, a chartered accountant.

Now, I was suspicious though I didn't say anything.

One evening, when Dave was out with some mates for a pint, the phone rang. "Hello," I said casually. I wondered if it might be my sister calling to make plans for the weekend.

"Is Dave there?" asked a young female voice.

My hands trembled as I lit a cigarette. Fortunately, I'd been a hairdresser since I was seventeen, so I knew how to keep my cool.

"He's just stepped out for a moment." I paused. "Who's calling, please?"

"It's his sister, Maureen," she replied in a high-pitched little voice.

It must have sounded ridiculous even to her.

Later, I gave myself credit for not having a go at her. Instead, I slammed down the receiver. When Dave came home, we had a row, and I said I wanted a divorce.

What hurt most of all was that she knew his sister's name.

Now, almost six years later, I felt as though it were happening all over again.

It was silly to feel that way. After all, Dave must have had dozens—well, let's say some—girlfriends since we'd split up. It was just that I hadn't seen him with any of them.

In fact, until he'd wandered into my salon four months earlier, I hadn't seen him in five years.

And it wasn't as though I was lonely. I was seeing a handsome, successful man, someone who cared about me and my career. In fact, he believed in Luxor more than I did.

Dave's love affairs were no concern of mine, and I was glad of it.

I curled into a fetal position in the empty bed. I wished Butler were there. His purr and the warmth of his body pressed against mine would have been a comfort.

***

On Friday afternoon, Jack rang me at Luxor.

"I've set a date for the transfer, Mandy," he said jubilantly. "Two weeks from today."

"Oh, brilliant." I hoped I sounded as excited as he wanted me to be.

"I thought you'd be keen. Let's go shopping this weekend."

"For what?" What in the world did shopping have to do with the transfer?

"For Luxor II, of course. I know you'll want to get in touch with the artist about the murals, but you can buy furniture and such in the meantime."

"Before I buy the salon?"

"It's as good as yours, and it'll take a few weeks for the items to be delivered anyway. Come on, Mandy. Enjoy this moment. You've earned it."

"You're sweet," I said. "I've got to run; a client's coming in a few minutes, but yes, let's celebrate."

"I'll bring a bottle of bubbly to your house tonight."

Betty cast a glance in my direction as I replaced the receiver. "Good news?"

"We've set a date for the transfer."

She smiled. "Congratulations, love. That's exciting."

"Thanks."

She returned to the salon's diary, and I realized she was giving me privacy.

After work, as I walked to my car, I heard someone call my name. A woman with short, blonde hair stood in front of a pub, waving at me.

"Nancy!" I cried, coming to an abrupt halt. "It's lovely to see you." I seldom saw clients outside of work, and Nancy was one of my favorites.

"I'm so glad you walked by," she said. "I took your boyfriend's advice about what to say to the chief of copy. Well, he liked the work I did on one brief, and he's given me another. I'm actually having a drink with some of the copywriters now."

"That's brilliant, love," I said. "Good for you."

"Thanks," she said. "And please tell your bloke. If it hadn't been for him, I would never have taken that step."

Her eyes were shining, and despite the grey sky and damp air, she looked younger than she had in years.

"He's all right," I said with a smile, "and I know he'll be pleased when I tell him."

I walked away feeling a bit lighter. The encounter was a reminder of how lucky I was to have someone like Jack in my life.

Jack and I had champagne that night. The next day, we selected some leather-upholstered chairs for Luxor II.

On Sunday evening, Dave dropped off the kids. They'd simply run out to meet him on Friday, so this was the first time I'd seen him since the recital. I'd made up my mind I wouldn't mention the recital or his girlfriend when I saw him. After all, it was none of my business whom he dated as long as she was fair to the kids. I would treat him with the friendly indifference ex-spouses should reserve for each other. Perhaps I would be a bit cooler than I had been in recent months.

Dave was supposed to drop off the kids at four. He appeared five minutes early. The kids ran upstairs as soon as I opened the door, leaving us to face each other on the threshold. He smiled uncertainly, hands in his pockets.

"Hi, Dave, come in," I said.

"Thanks, Mandy."

Once in the hallway, he stood awkwardly with his hands in his pockets.

"Quite talented, our little pianist," he said finally.

He would mention the recital. Did he want me to bring up his young girlfriend? I wouldn't rise to the bait.

"She's good," I said coolly. "Now I'd better see what she and Sam are up to." I stepped toward the staircase.

"Mandy, wait a moment."

I paused. What did he want now?

"I didn't get to speak to you at the recital or even the other night, but I wanted to ask you about your other salon."

"The transfer's in two weeks." I couldn't believe he wanted to know.

"Mandy, that's wonderful. Congratulations."

His eyes were bright, and he seemed genuinely happy for me, so I relented a bit.

"Thanks, Dave," I said quietly.

He glanced down at his shoes and then up at me almost shyly. "I've got some news of my own."

Now it was coming. No doubt he was going to marry the wretched girl.

"What is it?" I asked more coldly than I had intended.

"I saw Tim Lyons the other day. You know, the guitarist from Kodkod."

I nodded. Kodkod was a rock band that had had its heyday around or just after Serval's peak. But unlike Serval, they'd kept recording and touring.

"He came into the shop the other day. We hadn't seen each other in years, and we ended up getting a drink when I got off work. We talked a lot, but anyway, it seems their drummer has moved on, and he offered me the gig. I'll still be at the shop for the time being, but I'll be rehearsing with them and then recording and going on tour when the time comes. Apparently, they've got a massive fanbase in Sweden."

"Dave, that's marvelous!" I cried. He was so talented, it was criminal to think of him not drumming.

I was so beside myself to think of him playing music again that I threw my arms around his neck.

He smelled of soap and himself, but not, I noticed, tobacco.

Then I realized I was embracing him. Embarrassed, I stepped back.

"You—you've given up smoking," I stammered.

Dave chuckled. "Two weeks and three days now."

Then he cleared his throat. "I was wondering if you wanted to get a drink. To celebrate your good news and mine."

I opened my mouth to say yes. I closed it when I remembered the girl at the recital.

"Thanks, Dave, but Jack will be ringing me soon," I said finally. It wasn't a lie; he called every night.

Smiling, he studied the carpet and then looked up again, his eyes oddly moist.

"Goodbye, Manda," he said quietly.

He'd only ever called me that name during our most private moments. Certainly, he hadn't called me that in the five years we'd been divorced.

His fingers grazed my cheek. I knew I should respond, say something, but I was frozen to the carpet.

He turned then and walked through the door.

I almost walked after him.

Twenty-Four

I was relieved when a couple clients canceled that Tuesday. It freed me up to make a few calls in regards to Luxor II. I left the bankers and lawyers to Jack, but there was Connie, Lucas's ex-girlfriend, who might paint the salon's murals, and Lila, Elsie's Egyptologist friend, who would ensure they were historically accurate.

Robbie was with me at the desk as I dialed Connie's number. Betty was at the back having a quick lunch, and Rose was busy with a client, so he was looking after the front.

"I hope she's still at this number," I remarked, twirling the phone's cord with one finger. "I don't know what I'll do if I can't reach her."

"Get another artist then," said Robbie airily as he doodled a pharaoh in the diary's margins.

It was maddening, him being flippant at a time like this.

I slammed down the receiver. "It's not that simple!" I said. "I don't know that many artists, let alone anyone else who draws Egyptians."

Robbie raised his head from the diary and then one eyebrow. He would make a funny pharaoh.

"Don't shoot the messenger, darlin'." Once again, he studied the diary.

"If you can't reach her, maybe your Egyptologist friend knows someone," he said after a pause.

"Thanks, Robbie!" I exclaimed. I couldn't believe I hadn't thought of it.

"It gets overwhelming sometimes, planning one salon and running another," I added.

"It seems to me as though you just about handle Luxor I," he said.

He scurried away before I could reply.

Bloody cheek. Maybe Jack was right: I needed to be firmer with my staff.

I redialed Connie's number. As the phone rang, I wondered if Lila knew artists who drew Egyptian-style figures. It was a good idea, but being an Egyptologist didn't mean she knew artists, let alone those who specialized in painting pharaohs and the half-human, half-animal gods they'd worshipped—

"Hello?" inquired a female voice.

"Oh, hello, Connie, it's Mandy Wilt," I replied. "I need your expertise."

Quickly, I described my plans for Luxor II. She was enthusiastic, and we agreed to meet in Bath in three weeks, just after the transfer. We'd tour the salon and discuss its décor over lunch.

Then I called Lila at her office at the University of Bristol. To my surprise, she answered. She was also excited about Luxor II, and she agreed to join Connie and me when we met in Bath.

"Excellent," she said crisply before we rang off. "The world needs another Egyptian-themed salon."

As I replaced the receiver, my spirits lifted. Connie's and Lila's enthusiasm was contagious. I was running a successful salon, and I would soon be opening its sister salon with the help of two brilliant women and the kindest, most generous man in London. Making plans for the salon's décor had made it all real.

A little peal of laughter sounded behind me. Half-turning, I glimpsed Rose laughing with her client, a young girl a few years older than herself. Her eyes were bright as she trimmed the girl's hair and chatted animatedly with her. She had come out of her shell in the last few months, and clients loved her.

Really, I was lucky to have such a fabulous staff. Robbie could be cheeky now and again, but he was a talented hairdresser, and his heart was in the right place. Rose was a treasure, and Betty had quickly proven herself an asset. There had been that to-do with Emmy that I still didn't like to think about, but even that had worked out for the best as she had gotten a place out of it and so had Betty.

Staff. I'd have to hire at least one stylist, maybe two for Luxor II. I couldn't be there more than one or two days a week, not without neglecting my own clients. How many did I need? And how could I recruit them and make sure they met my standards without spending days, even weeks, in Bath?

Suddenly, opening Luxor II had become very real.

On Thursday night, Jack and I had dinner at San Lorenzo while Mrs. Jones looked after Katie and Sam. I'd forgotten to tell him about Nancy's triumph over the weekend, so over plates of spaghetti, I told him.

"Apparently, they want her to do more writing for them," I said. "And it's all down to you for giving her the right advice."

Jack gave a quick nod of satisfaction. "Glad to hear it."

"And it's a reminder of how lucky I am to have the most generous man in London in my life."

Jack's blue eyes shone as they met mine over his champagne flute.

"I like helping talented people make the most of themselves. And I'm sitting opposite the most beautiful woman in London—and one of its most original businesswomen."

He lifted my hand to his lips.

I held his gaze for an instant before toying with my pasta. "Speaking of business, I made some plans for Luxor II this week," I said. I described my calls to Connie and Lila.

Again, he nodded in approval. "Excellent."

"There's just one thing. Hiring new stylists while running the first salon. I'm not sure how I'll do it all at once."

"How did you do it the first time around?"

"With Luxor? Well, Robbie and I worked together at my previous salon. I brought him with me, and we each came with our own clients. Emmy and Rose responded to an advert. I met them, spoke with their references, and hired them."

"And you couldn't do the same with Luxor II?"

"I could hire a junior that way. But I'd need one or two seasoned hairdressers, someone who could bring her own clientele to the business. And I don't know any stylists in Bath."

Jack's eyes narrowed in thought. "I see."

He paused. "Of course, I've got no experience with the salon business, but it seems to me you've got to find the best there is. Could you visit the top salons in Bath and persuade one or two of their stylists to work with you?"

Was he mad? I swallowed more champagne than I meant to and coughed.

"That's not how it's done!" I exclaimed when I finished coughing.

He looked puzzled. "But didn't you persuade Robbie to go to Luxor with you?"

I sighed. "Yes, but no. I mean I did, but it's different. We were mates; we worked together. It's not the same as going into someone else's salon and trying to get one of the stylists to work with you. I know I wouldn't want anyone doing it to me."

Now Jack sighed. "It's business, Mandy. It's how it's done in most industries. You want the best talent, you've got to go after it, and the best people are generally already working for someone else."

"You're right," I said because he was.

"Of course, I could advertise," I continued slowly. "An advert in the nationals and the Bath and Bristol papers. Wanted: hairdresser with own clientele for chair in new Bath salon. I'd have to make it very exciting to attract the right people." I paused. "I could hire one, maybe two, stylists and then a junior as time went on."

"A very sound plan," said Jack, smiling. "I'm proud of you, Mandy."

Almost shyly, I returned his smile. I felt like a little girl when he praised me like that.

I sipped my champagne. Writing an advert that people wanted to read—now that was outside my ken. Who did I know who could do it? Elsie would do it if I asked her, but she was busy with her column and her book and her cats.

Then I had an inspiration.

"Nancy could do it!" I cried. "As a little freelance project. And she could write the adverts for Luxor II as well. It would be some extra income for her and a feather in her cap."

Jack's eyes were brighter than ever as he placed a hand over mine.

"That's what I love about you, Mandy," he said. "You've got a head on your shoulders, but you've got a heart, too. Let's go to Paris to celebrate once you've launched Luxor II."

"That would be lovely," I said. "I've not been in years."

Thirteen years to be exact. Dave had taken me soon after we started going out.

Jack pressed my hand, and for the second time that week, I felt as though things were happening just as they ought.

***

That Saturday evening, as I rummaged through the day's mail, I found a postcard. It was a photo of Big Ben, the sort an American would buy. Who would send a Londoner a Big Ben postcard? Smiling, I flipped it over.

I'd know the printed capitals anywhere.

MANDY,

SOMETHING HAS COME UP, AND I WON'T BE ABLE TO TAKE THE KIDS NEXT WEEK-END. REALLY SORRY—WILL MAKE IT UP TO YOU SOON.

YOURS EVER,

DAVE

"Something has come up." I snorted. I knew very well what that meant. He had plans with that Chrissy, and he didn't have the bollocks to tell me.

I would have had more respect for him if he had.

I stomped into the front room, where Sam was watching *The Fame Game* on the telly. At my approach, he started, his eyes wide with alarm.

"What's wrong, Mum?" he asked.

Poor boy. He wasn't used to seeing me furious.

"Nothing, love," I said lightly. "I wonder, though, if you wouldn't mind going upstairs for a bit. I've got to make a call."

He shrugged and bounced off the sofa, shutting off the telly as he passed. Poor boy, he was very keen on the program, but he was putting a good face on it.

I dialed Dave's number. He should be off work by now. Of course, he might be out with his mates or that Chrissy or rehearsing with the band—

There were a few rings before someone answered. "Hello?" said a young female voice.

So she was living there now, at least on the weekend.

It was impossible not to think of that other call before our divorce.

"Hello, is Dave Wilt there?" I asked calmly. I might have been a secretary making a call for her boss.

"He's not here at the moment," replied the girl. "May I take a message?"

Oh, she was brazen in her own little way, playing the secretary role herself. Now she had asked for it.

"Yes," I said more firmly. "This is his ex-wife, Mandy Wilt. Can you please tell him that I received his postcard? And you might add that he should be able to do a better job of explaining why he can't be a father to his children."

There was silence on the other end.

"Is that quite clear?" I made my voice hard like I had the day I sacked Emmy.

"Yes," said the girl in a smaller voice than ever.

"All right, then. See he gets the message."

I rang off and put my head in my hands. I had thought I'd feel better after having a go at her.

I didn't.

Twenty-Five

Later that night, Jack called.

"How about a weekend in Paris, Mandy?" he asked. His voice was jauntier than usual.

"Lovely!" I replied. I was still smarting from the exchange with Chrissy, and I had to work at sounding bright and animated.

"How about next weekend to be exact?"

"Jack, I'd love to, but I've got to think of the kids."

"Doesn't their father have them next week?"

I sighed. "He was supposed to." I explained the strange little post-card and my conversation with Chrissy.

Jack snorted, and somehow the sound reminded me of an angry bull.

"Is that all the explanation he could give?"

"It's obviously something he didn't want me to know."

"But we know what it is." I'd never heard Jack that sarcastic before. Oh, why couldn't he drop it?

"He's never done anything like this before, so there must be a good explanation." I couldn't believe I was defending Dave. I'd wanted to throttle him a couple hours earlier.

"Anyhow," I continued, "you know Saturdays are off limits for me unless I give my clients a couple months' notice. It's one of our busiest days."

He only hesitated for a few seconds. "Couldn't you just take Sunday and Monday? We could leave Saturday evening and return late Monday."

Now we were going in circles.

"But don't you see? I've got no one to look after Katie and Sam. Dave's not available."

This time the pause was longer. "They couldn't stay with your sister?"

I laughed. "Kate? Watch the kids for the weekend? When it might interfere with their tennis or Jennifer's pony club? Don't hold your breath."

"Well, you'll see I don't give up so easily, Mandy. After we've finalized things with Luxor II, I'm taking you to Paris for a week."

We said goodbye, and I smiled slightly as I replaced the receiver. He was so persistent, bless him. Funny how someone could be so sharp in one way and understand so little in another.

***

On Monday afternoon, Elsie rang me at home.

"How are you, love?" I said.

"I'm all right. I was calling to check on you and the kids." Her little American voice sounded concerned.

"Funny you should ask," I replied with a laugh and told her about Dave's mysterious postcard and Jack's invitation to Paris.

"How about the kids come to ours for the weekend?" she asked when I finished.

"To you and Alec?"

"Yes. We'll pick them up on Saturday and make sure they're at school Monday morning. That way, you and Jack can have your weekend in Paris."

"Really?" I exclaimed. "Elsie, you are a sweetheart!"

"Alec and I will love it. He'll have someone in the house who likes football as much as he does, and you know, we only see my niece and nephew once a year and his brother's kids less than that. So it'll be fun."

I was grateful, but I couldn't help feeling sorry for her. I knew she missed having her own family.

Jack and I had lunch at a pub on Tuesday.

"So it looks as though Paris is possible after all," I said brightly as we took our seats.

Jack lifted his eyebrows slightly as he sipped his Guinness. "I told you it was nonnegotiable."

"I mean this weekend. Elsie and Alec are happy to have the kids from Saturday through Monday. We can go!"

Jack set down his pint glass, folded his arms, and gazed steadily at me. "I can't, Mandy. I've got business in Birmingham."

My eyebrows drew together. "But you didn't mention that on Saturday."

"I didn't know about it then. But something's come up with a property I've acquired—a tenant who won't leave—and I've got to see about it."

Sipping my chardonnay, I studied the wooden table top. Why did he have so many bloody properties all over the country?

His hand was atop mine.

"I'm sorry, Mandy," he said more gently than usual. "It's business, though, and I know you understand that."

He paused. "We'll have all more reason to celebrate after the transfer."

Smiling, I raised my head, and his hand pressed mine.

"Speaking of your salons, Nancy—your client—did some wonderful work on the advert for Luxor II," he said. "I asked to have her put on the brief when I rang her agency about the series. Look at this mock-up."

Sporting an Egyptian-style headdress, blonde woman occupied a throne.

Why be queen for a day when you could be a legend?

Luxor II, North Parade Passage, Bath

"That's brilliant," I said. "I'm so glad she's finally writing for them. It's a shame it's taken them so long to see how talented she is." I paused. "It was a good move, really, having her do the work through her job at the agency and not as a freelancer."

"She'll be account manager before it's all said and done," said Jack gleefully.

I wrinkled my nose. "But what if she's happy being a copywriter? I mean, it's what she's wanted all these years."

"But she's a bright woman," said Jack. "Why shouldn't she want to get to the top of her profession?"

Our food arrived, and we talked of other things. As I ate my chicken salad, I wondered how many times our plans would change because of Jack's business or mine.

***

That night, I rang Elsie to tell her about our change of plans.

"Come anyway," she said. "All three of you. It would be good to see you, and I know Alec will be absolutely deflated if he can't have his kickabout with Sam."

So, on Saturday evening, the three of us drove to Foxgrove Lodge, Elsie and Alec's house in Kent. It was an impressive three-story Queen Anne home with its dormer windows. Apparently, it had once been some noble family's hunting lodge. They'd sold it off in the nineteenth century when they'd fallen on hard times.

After Serval broke up, I'd wondered if Elsie and Alec would manage to keep Foxgrove. But they both loved the house, and so rather than give it up, they'd sold off a couple of Alec's cars and retrenched in all sorts of ways. They took it well, bless them; sometimes, I think they even enjoyed frugality. Elsie was proud of shopping at Marks and Sparks, and since they were both happy with simple meals, they didn't spend a lot on food. And Alec made just enough money from Nest Egg to make keeping Foxgrove possible.

The five of us ate by candlelight in Foxgrove's big dining room. Elsie's roast beef and Yorkshire puddings were delicious washed down with Burgundy, and because they'd spent so many happy hours at

Foxgrove, the kids felt comfortable asking for seconds. I even allowed myself a slice of Elsie's chocolate cake.

After dinner, we all sat in the conversation pit in front of the fireplace in the library. It was an impressive room with its inlaid bookcases filled with Alec and Elsie's books. It suited them, this cozy room, and I knew they loved nothing more than spending hours reading here. I was glad they'd kept the conversation pit even though lots of other people had built over theirs; it was made for evenings like these.

The children's faces glowed in the firelight. They were far more comfortable with Elsie and Alec than they were with my family, and they chatted freely. Sam and Alec discussed Chelsea's and Leeds' prospects, and Katie told Elsie stories about Lemon and Minty.

"Lemon sniffs Minty's bum," said Katie. "Then Minty walks away with her tail in the air. She looks really annoyed." She paused. "I think Lemon likes winding her up."

Elsie laughed. "I expect so. You'll meet our latest fosters tomorrow. I'd introduce you now, but I expect they're tired."

"And they're not the only ones," I said as Sam stifled a yawn. "You can kiss Aunt Elsie and Uncle Alec and off to bed with you."

After the kids went upstairs, Alec uncorked a second bottle of Burgundy and filled our glasses. It was cozy sitting there by the fireplace with them. For the second time that evening, it occurred to me that they felt more like family than my family did.

"Thank you," I said suddenly, "for having us this weekend. It's been lovely, and it's just good for the kids to be around people who love them after Dave's walkabout."

I'd had two glasses of wine. That, and the fact that I'd known them and they'd known Dave for a long time loosened my tongue.

"Of all the selfish things to do," I continued. "It's bad enough that he's got a girlfriend young enough to be his daughter. He has to go away with her the weekend he's got Katie and Sam—and he doesn't even have the guts to tell me about it."

Alec stared grimly at the wall above my head. I regretted speaking so frankly in front of him. They were mates, after all, and I didn't want to put him in an awkward position.

Elsie's blue eyes were large and sympathetic in the firelight. She glanced fleetingly at Alec as if she were asking him a question.

He nodded slightly.

Elsie leaned forward slightly across the coffee table. She opened her mouth, shut it, then opened it again as if she weren't sure how to begin.

"Mandy," she said quietly. "Dave isn't going away with anyone this weekend."

Again, she hesitated as if she were searching for the right words.

"He's having surgery on Monday," she said finally. "He has cancer."

Twenty-Six

Apart from the crackling of the fire, the library was silent. My hand reached across the coffee table, fumbling for an ashtray.

Then I remembered Elsie and Alec didn't smoke.

Neither did I.

Somehow, Elsie was beside me, her arms around my shoulders.

"Drink this," said Alec's voice.

My right hand held a shot glass. The whiskey burned in my throat. I coughed and sputtered.

Elsie, now back on the loveseat, stared at me with large eyes. "I'm sorry, Mandy. I should never have told you like that."

Poor little thing. It was like her to blame herself.

"No, no, love. You were as gentle as you could be." I paused. "But why didn't Dave tell me himself, the bastard?"

This time it was Alec who replied. "He didn't want to worry you or the children," he said quietly.

"But I had no way of knowing!" I cried. "I thought he had some dirty weekend planned with that girl."

"What girl?" asked Alec sharply. "Dave's not had a girlfriend in months."

"But—who's that girl he's always with?"

Alec's eyebrows drew together, and Elsie's blue eyes were bewildered. Was it possible they knew Dave had cancer, but not that he had a girlfriend?

"He showed up at Katie's recital with some blonde," I said impatiently. "She looked about sixteen. Apparently, she's at his flat sometimes. Her name is Chrissy."

"Oh, she's not his girlfriend," said Alec. "She's his niece."

"His niece!" I exclaimed. It was my day for repeating what people said to me.

Elsie nodded vigorously. "Yes, Chrissy's eighteen, just finishing her A-levels. She'll be starting at one of the polytechnics in the autumn, and she'll be staying with Dave then. She wants to be a teacher."

I was silent. I'd known Dave's sister, Maureen, had two children, a boy and a girl, but we'd only seen Maureen, Frank, and the kids a handful of times during the six years we were married. It wasn't that Dave and Maureen didn't get on; it's just that they'd never been close.

"The last time I saw Chrissy, she was about eleven," I said slowly. I remembered a quiet, slender girl with blonde plaits. She'd glanced shyly at me when we were round his parents' for a family party.

"It's understandable you wouldn't recognize her," said Elsie. "Not after all that time."

"But why didn't Dave tell me she was his niece?" I exclaimed. "It would have made it so much easier."

"Did you talk about her with him?" asked Elsie.

"No. But what was I to think when he showed up at Katie's recital with a pretty blonde? And the kids mentioned that she had stayed at the flat. He might have introduced us."

Elsie bit her lip. Even in the dim light, I could tell her eyes were moist.

Alec sighed. Then he spoke more gently to me than he ever had before.

"Mandy, Dave would have liked to talk to you more. About Chrissy and other things. But whenever he tried—he said it never seemed to be the right time."

I stared past them. Behind us, a log snapped in half and collapsed with a thud.

I had been too busy, too important, too proud to talk with Dave all those times he had asked me for a drink. I hadn't given him a chance to tell me about Maureen or Chrissy. Or his cancer.

The room had gone silent, the kind of silence you could hear.

"How sick is he?" I asked finally.

"It's thyroid cancer," replied Elsie. "He'll have surgery on Monday, and then the surgeons will see if he needs more treatment."

"He said it wasn't particularly bad as cancers go," said Alec.

As if that was supposed to reassure me. "He would say that." I paused. "But why couldn't he just tell me? Even if he'd just said he was sick. He ought to have known I'd assume the worst."

Again, Alec was quiet. "He obviously preferred to have you angry than to worry you."

That was Dave all over. He'd never wanted to upset me or the kids. Look at what he'd done when Bruiser died.

"And his operation's Monday," I said slowly.

Elsie nodded.

"Would you—could someone—call me when it's over? To let me know if he's all right?"

"We won't be at hospital with him," said Alec.

"But Chrissy will," said Elsie. "I'm sure she wouldn't mind calling you."

I felt my cheeks redden. "But I had a go at her last weekend when I rang Dave's flat."

Alec shrugged.

"I'm sure she'll understand," said Elsie gently.

I nodded. Suddenly, my eyes were very heavy.

I rose from the sofa. "Well, I expect I'll turn in now," I announced. "Thanks for a lovely evening. The roast beef was delicious, and I don't remember the last time I had whiskey."

Elsie made as if to follow me. "Are you all right, Mandy? Would you like a cup of tea or something?"

"I'm all right, love. Good night."

I bounced up the stairs as if I'd just come back from the cinema. But once I was in my room, I quickly donned my nightgown. I burrowed beneath the duvet in a fetal position, grateful for its warmth. It was a long time before I fell asleep.

***

The next day, I was able to put on a good face for the kids. We all admired the pair of tabbies Elsie was fostering in one of their spare rooms and paid homage to their own cats, Hercules and Jane. Alec played football with Sam in the back garden, and Elsie showed Katie how to make chocolate chip cookies.

"An American delicacy," she said, grinning. "And these are almost as good as my mom's."

While Elsie and Alec entertained the kids, I called Dave's flat on the phone in the library.

"Hello?" said a young female voice after the second ring.

There was no way around it.

"Hi, Chrissy, it's Mandy Wilt," I began.

There was silence on the line. Perhaps the poor girl thought I was going to have a go at her again.

"Hi," she said finally in a little voice.

"I'm sorry I had a go at you last week, love," I said. "I—I thought you were someone else altogether."

I paused. "You see, it'd been so long since I'd seen you. And the last time I saw you—at your grandparents' house—you were still a little girl. When I saw you with Dave at the piano recital, I got the wrong idea."

My palms were sweaty as my fingers toyed with the phone cord. I'd never felt so foolish.

"That's okay," said the polite little voice.

Once again, I gulped.

"Thank you, love." I paused. "Chrissy, I know about Dave's surgery. Could you call me after the operation tomorrow? Just to let me know if he's all right?"

The line was silent again. I hoped she wasn't upset because I knew. Worse still, what if she told Dave and he took it out on Alec and Elsie?

"The kids don't know," I said quietly.

"The operation is scheduled for eleven," said Chrissy. "Where should I call you?"

"Well, I don't work Mondays, so home. Wait, I forgot. This Monday afternoon, I'll be in Bath."

I rummaged through my bag and gave her the estate agent's number. "But if it's after three, you can leave a message at my house. I've got an answering machine."

"Thank you."

"No, thank you, Chrissy," I said warmly. "And again, I'm sorry about the way I acted last week. I had no right to do that."

"That's all right, Aunt Mandy."

After saying goodbye, I replaced the receiver and sank onto the loveseat. The scent of woodsmoke lingered, but with no fire in the grate, the room was cold.

In fewer than twenty-four hours, Jack and I would be on our way to Bath to sign the papers for Luxor II.

And in just over twenty-four, a surgeon would be cutting Dave's throat.

Twenty-Seven

We left Foxgrove Lodge at six the following morning. In the backseat, Katie and Sam dozed in their school uniforms. At a traffic light, I glanced at them in the rearview mirror. Katie was slumped against Sam's shoulder, her cheeks slightly flushed under her blonde pigtails. Sam's lips were parted, so he appeared childlike despite his blue and green plaid blazer.

I had an urge to pull over right then and there and take them in my arms. But I forced myself to drive on. They had to be at school by eight after all.

Normally, when I dropped Sam at school, I just waved goodbye to him. But today was different somehow. I climbed out of the car and embraced him, holding him a few seconds longer than was normal for an almost-eleven-year-old.

Around us, on the pavement, other students were arriving. Some stepped out of cars; others came on foot, chatting amongst themselves.

"Good morning, Mrs. Wilt," said a voice.

A tall, thin boy stood behind us on the pavement. His ginger hair stood up a bit, and his freckled face smiled.

"Hi, Gareth, love, you all right?" Gareth was Sam's best mate and my favorite of his friends.

Red-faced, Sam squirmed away from my embrace. "Bye, Mum," he muttered.

"Love you, darling. Lovely to see you, Gareth."

I climbed back in the car. Poor boy. I'd embarrassed him in front of his friend, perhaps the whole school. I'd try to be more sensitive in the future.

From the backseat, Katie regarded me with her large blue eyes.

"Mummy, why did you hug Sam for so long?"

"Sometimes, you just feel like hugging people." I started the Cavalier. "If you like, I'll give you an extra big hug when we get to your school."

Katie yawned. "You don't have to."

She was seven years old, and it was already starting. I wouldn't overreact.

"I know I don't have to. I want to because I love you."

She was silent. When we came to a stoplight, I studied her in the rearview mirror. She was gazing out the window as though I hadn't spoken.

When the light changed, I drove on.

"Was that why you hugged Daddy that day?"

I inhaled sharply. Ahead of me, a blue Ford Escort was stopped at an intersection. I slammed on the brakes just in time.

"Which day was that?" I was surprised at how even my voice was.

"The last time he brought us home."

"Oh, that," I said lightly. "Well, your dad had good news that day. He'd been offered the job with the band, and I was happy for him."

I paused. "If you've known people a long time, you're very glad when things go well for them. So you hug them."

Katie seemed to accept this, for we rode in silence for a few minutes.

"Do you hug Jack?" she asked when I pulled up in front of her school.

"All the time," I replied. "And now I'm going to hug you."

I held her tightly. She squirmed away faster than Sam had and ran up to the school without a backward glance.

Back at the house, I drank two cups of instant coffee. For the second time in two days, I craved a cigarette. Instead, I donned a belted red dress and a black blazer and applied fresh red lipstick. I looked like a businesswoman, and that was what I was going to be.

At ten, Jack picked me up in his Mercedes. He looked distinguished in his grey suit, and his eyes crinkled at the corners as I climbed into the passenger seat.

"You look beautiful, Mandy. As though you could take on the world. I'm proud of you."

He kissed me, and because I felt guilty, I returned his kiss with more enthusiasm than I felt.

"Well, the sun's shining," he declared as he started the car. "An auspicious beginning for Luxor II. How was your weekend in Kent?"

"It was nice. It was lovely to see Elsie and Alec, and the kids had a great time."

"And you?"

Sometimes, he could be keen. I had to give him that much.

"Oh, Elsie's one of my best friends, and she and Alec wined and dined me . . ."

I hesitated. I should tell him the news about Dave. We'd been seeing each other for months, and we were going into business together. I could trust him. I should trust him.

"What happened, Mandy?"

I opened my mouth. But Dave. He hadn't wanted his own children to know.

"Nothing," I replied. "It's just that I was missing you. And nervous about today."

Jack took my hand and pressed it to his lips. His stubble tickled my fingers, but I resisted the urge to move my hand away.

"Well, I'm here now," he said. "And there's nothing to be nervous about. The transfer's a mere formality. All the hard work of negotiating's already been done." He paused. "Normally, you know, all of the papers can be sent through the post, but I thought it'd good for you—and a bit more momentous—to speak with the lawyers yourself."

I gulped. He'd gone to so much trouble on my behalf.

"How was Birmingham?" I asked.

"All right. I was able to sort out the problem with the contractor and the tenant . . ."

I tried to listen, but my mind kept wandering. Scenes from the past played through my mind in no particular order.

I remembered Dave the day Sam was born. The wonder in his eyes as he held his son for the first time.

Then I recalled him lifting Katie into the air when she was a baby and her delighted giggle when he brought her back down again.

There was our wedding day. My mum hadn't been much for churchgoing, so I was nervous about walking down the aisle at his parents' parish church. As I dressed, I talked feverishly to my bridesmaids. They must have thought I'd taken speed or something.

But as I stood at the back of the church, I saw Dave standing by the altar. His eyes smiled into mine, and I knew then that I would be all right.

We would be all right.

The day I'd met him. It was 1972, I was twenty-one, and he'd come into the salon where I worked on the King's Road. As I trimmed his hair, he made me giggle. The salon's proprietress, a tall woman with fishy grey eyes, gave me a cold stare. But I didn't care. That evening, we had dinner at a little bistro just around the corner. And our first kiss later that night.

The first time we went to bed.

The time we'd gone for a country walk near Hastings, where he'd grown up. I wore heels—I was London born and bred, and I'd never spent much time in the country before. Or cared to, really. But it had been all right until we came to a little brook. There was no way around it, only through it.

"We'll have to turn back," I said.

"I can't take you anywhere," Dave declared.

Then he lifted me into his arms and carried me across the stream. I giggled, protesting all the way.

As he set me down, I felt someone watching us. I turned to see a thin woman on a tall brown horse. She was middle-aged, and with her tweed jacket, breeches, and riding crop, she looked very posh.

"Good afternoon," she said in a clipped voice.

"Hello," I said, flushing. How silly she must think me in my heels as she sat there looking so capable with her riding crop.

"Good afternoon," said Dave.

She nodded and urged her horse forward. As they passed, an indulgent smile spread over her features.

I felt then that all the world was on our side. Even this woman in tweed, probably even her horse, approved of us.

That night, Dave asked me to marry him.

Dave smiling uncertainly that November day when he'd appeared at Luxor.

And the last time I'd seen him. How he'd looked when he touched my cheek and called me Manda. The sight of his back as he'd walked away. I'd wanted to go after him.

Why I hadn't I?

"Penny for your thoughts."

I started. Jack was beside me, his hands on the wheel.

"I was thinking how lovely it will be to have an excuse to come to Bath," I said.

Jack nodded. "Yes, you'll have to come out regularly. Just to ensure it's up to your standards."

I imagined myself taking a white glove to surfaces and scrutinizing the stylists' work.

It sounded like a lot of effort.

I glanced at my watch. Ten-thirty. Dave's operation was scheduled for eleven, and we were meeting the solicitors and estate agent at half-past one.

We had lunch at a nice pub, just around the corner from the estate agent and what would soon be Luxor II. As Jack pointed out, there was no point in arriving too early at the estate agent's office.

"So you can consider this an early celebration, Mandy," said Jack. "But, of course, we'll celebrate properly later with champagne. Santé."

His glass of Burgundy clinked against my glass of chardonnay. I flashed him a smile and took a bigger sip than I'd planned.

My steak and kidney pud was delicious although I barely tasted it; I was eating so quickly.

Fortunately, Jack put my nerves down to the transfer.

He placed a hand on mine and smiled reassuringly. "It's natural to be nervous before a step of this magnitude, Mandy. But you're more than up to it; I promise."

He was so kind.

"I'm so glad Nancy's been promoted to copywriter," I said. "She's wanted it for so long."

Jack's face broke into a smile. "Yes, she earned it with her talent and determination." He paused. "I've been thinking she might do some writing for my firm. Not copywriting, I don't need that, but some public relations. It would strengthen her CV."

"That's so sweet of you." With his belief in people, he would make a good father. If his children were the sort to make something of themselves, that is.

We lingered in the pub, and I allowed myself a second glass of wine. After all, it was a special occasion.

We arrived at the estate agent's at a quarter past one.

The receptionist knew us. "Good morning, Mrs. Wilt, Mr. Slayton," she said.

"Hello, Janet," I replied. "Has anyone rung for me?"

She shook her head. "No, I'm sorry."

Jack shot me a look out of the corner of his eye. "Are you expecting a call, Mandy?"

"Possibly. An old friend's in hospital, and another friend said she'd call. When the operation was over."

It was the truth.

Jack nodded as if this were to be expected.

We took our seats in the small waiting area. I'd just opened a copy of *Woman's Own* when the phone rang.

I leapt to my feet.

"Hello, Gosford and Park Estate Agents," said Janet. "Hello, Mr. Chatsworth. Yes, I'll let them know."

She hung up. "That was Mr. Chatsworth, the other party's solicitor. He's running a bit behind and sends his apologies. He'll be here by half-past two at the latest."

An entire hour behind schedule. Even more time to await Chrissy's call.

"Thanks, Janet," said Jack.

"Would you like some tea?" she asked.

Jack looked at me, and I shook my head.

I returned to *Woman's Own* and began an article about summer starters. I stopped when I realized I'd read the same page three times.

Mr. Park, the young estate agent, and Mr. Brent, our solicitor, arrived. Janet showed us into a private room with a long table and offered us tea. This time, I accepted. It would be something to do.

Mr. Park and Mr. Brent played golf together. Their club reopened in April.

"Do you play golf, Mrs. Wilt?" asked Mr. Brent.

I shook my head. "I've never been much for sports."

"You must come with us sometime, you and Mr. Slayton. Very nice restaurant at the clubhouse."

And I pretended to be interested in golf. I knew when to smile and ask questions. After all, I'd been a hairdresser for years.

Out in the lobby, the phone rang. This time, I forced myself to stay in my seat.

Footsteps sounded in the corridor. I held my breath.

Janet knocked on the door before she opened it. "Mrs. Wilt? There's a call for you. A Chrissy."

I rose. "Excuse me."

I followed Janet to the front desk, where she handed me the phone.

"Hello?" I said.

"Hi, Aunt Mandy, it's Chrissy." Her voice was young, tiny.

"Hello, love. How are you?"

"All right. And you?"

Why didn't she just tell me? Was she hesitating for a reason?

"Is anything the matter?"

"Uncle Dave's just come out of surgery. I spoke to the surgeon. He'll have to be in hospital for three days, but the doctor says he'll be fine."

"Oh, thank God." My voice broke. "Please give him my love. And thank you for calling, love."

In a daze, I handed the receiver back to Janet. Slowly, I walked back to the room where Jack, Mr. Park, and Mr. Brent all awaited Mr. Chatsworth.

I opened the door and stood in the doorway, looking at Jack.

"Is anything the matter?" asked Jack.

I shook my head.

He mustn't have believed me, for he rose and followed me into the corridor, closing the door behind him.

"Your friend—" he began.

"My friend's all right," I said quietly.

Then I burst into tears. "I never wanted a second salon," I sobbed. "One's enough for me, always has been."

My face was in my hands, and salty tears ran into my mouth. A proper businesswoman I must look.

Then Jack's arms were around me. "There, there," he said awkwardly. "No need to cry."

Twenty-Eight

My staff took the news better than I thought they would.

On Tuesday morning, before clients started arriving, I called a little meeting at the desk. Betty and Rose looked expectantly at me; Robbie raised one arched eyebrow.

"I have some news," I began.

Robbie's eyebrow crept an eighth of an inch higher. I hoped he wouldn't say, "I told you so."

It was going to sound foolish no matter how I said it. I took a deep breath.

"I decided not to go through with it," I said. "Luxor II, that is. No journeys to Bath for me. So you're stuck with me for the time being."

Robbie's face burst into a smile. His green eyes were soft, and for the first time in the nearly three years we'd worked together, I noticed his cheeks still had puppy fat.

Rose's dark eyes were concerned. "Is everything all right?"

"Are you all right?" asked Betty pointedly.

I nodded quickly. "Yes. But somehow, at the transfer, I realized it wasn't what I wanted. Having two salons."

Again, I took a deep breath. "What I love is cutting hair and being with clients." I paused. "And working with all of you."

Rose smiled shyly, and Betty's features softened.

"Well, as long as you're happy, love," said Betty. "That's the main thing." But I heard the relief in her voice.

"I am happy. That's why we should have a drink after work tonight. It's been ages since we've gone to the pub, and I think we should celebrate. If everyone's free, that is. Mrs. Jones can look after the kids for an extra hour or so."

"I'm free," said Rose.

"Me, too," said Betty. "Nat and Jason can fend for themselves for an hour."

Robbie yawned. "Yeah, I could have a drink."

His fingers turned the pages of the salon's diary, but his eyes were moist.

"Excellent," I said brightly. "How about the Chelsea Potter?"

There were nods, and then we went about our day. It had been months since we'd had a drink together after work, well before Betty started. November, if I remembered correctly.

I'd missed my odd little family.

Jack, too, took my decision surprisingly well.

"If your heart's not in it, there's no use for it," he said as we drove back to London after the transfer. "I'll find another tenant for the salon; Nancy can write the copy for the advert. We shouldn't have any trouble finding one—it's a prime location."

For he'd decided to buy the salon on his own. The solicitors had worked it out with the estate agent.

"But let's go to Paris, the two of us, this spring," he said.

And three weeks later, we did. At that point, Dave was well enough to take the children, and he and Chrissy were excited to have them for a long weekend. Robbie looked after the house and Lemon and Minty whilst we were away.

As the taxi sped away from Charles de Gaulle airport to the Westminster Hotel, I thought about a whirlwind holiday in Paris Dave and I had taken a few months after we'd started going out in 1972. I was twenty-one then, I was thirty-four now, and I hadn't been since. Paris had changed and so had I. It would be good to see it again.

Paris was beautiful in April. Of course, we saw some of the same sights. The gargoyles on Notre Dame were just as monstrous as I remembered, and I enjoyed seeing the *Mona Lisa* and the Venus de Milo at the Louvre just as much as I had on the first holiday, perhaps more. Or maybe it seemed all the more remarkable that I was in Paris seeing some of the world's greatest works of art.

Jack humored me and let an artist sketch my portrait in Montmartre just as one had in 72. We went shopping, too, just as Dave and I had on our holiday. But back in 1972, I'd been ecstatic to comb through the odd little shops in Pigalle. This time, Jack took me to the Chanel shop on Rue Cambon. The dresses and suits would never be me, but I bought Coco perfume for Betty, No. 19 for Rose, and a green silk scarf for Robbie.

And Jack insisted that we experience the city's best cuisine. We dined under crystal chandeliers at Le Train Bleu. The occasion seemed worthy of a dessert: in my case, crèpes Suzette flambéed at our table.

On our second night, after dinner, Jack and I stood on the balcony of our hotel suite. Below us was the Place Vendôme, its lights aglow in the darkness. I wore a strapless black satin cocktail dress, and Jack's arm was around my shoulder. Smoke from his cigar wafted past my nose.

How different it had been the first time. I'd hoped to try one of the posh restaurants, but I wanted to cry when we stopped outside a restaurant and read the menu on display. Or tried to.

"I can only understand a word here and there!" I cried. "I want to know what I'm eating." I'd only had a year of French at school as had Dave.

Dave's eyes sparkled as though he had a secret. "I've got a better idea."

He'd anticipated something like this, so, earlier in the day, he'd purchased a loaf of bread, some brie, and a bottle of cabernet sauvignon

We had a picnic near one of the lakes in the famous park, the Bois de Boulogne. We laughed all through dinner, but we really talked, too. Dave opened up to me far more than he had in the past. He wanted to keep working on his drumming; one day, he hoped to be as good as John Bonham or Keith Moon. And someday, he thought of producing.

"I'm not a songwriter," he said, almost shyly. "I'll leave that to Alec and the others. But I've got a feel for how things sound—how parts of a song come together."

We talked about our families, too. Dave was full of admiration for his parents. "I hope I can be half the father my dad was. No matter how tired he was, he always had time for us. Always."

We made short work of the bread and the cheese and the wine. Afterwards, we lay in the grass, Dave's arm around my shoulder. We lay there smoking and laughing and talking.

The wine must have made us louder than we should have been because some passersby frowned at us, including two old women.

"Ils sont fous," said the thinner of the two, a dour woman in a headscarf.

I knew that much French at least.

The plump one laughed indulgently. "Ah, non, cherie. Ils sont seulement jeunes et amoureux."

Jack's voice cut through my memory. "Look at it, Mandy. It seems made for us, doesn't it? For lovers?"

"Oh, yes," I replied.

For after all, this was what grown-up Paris was like.

We only had the two nights in Paris. I had to get back to Luxor, and Jack had business in Glasgow.

He gave me a lingering kiss when he dropped me off at the house in Ealing.

"We'll have more weekends like this, Mandy," he said. "And proper holidays, too. I'd love to see Rome with you."

The musky scent of Jack's aftershave lingered in the foyer after he left. I unpacked my suitcase and fed the kittens. He had his life, and I had mine. He didn't need me, but he wanted the best for me, and we could enjoy each other's company.

Perhaps that's what being in love was like for adults.

In the early evening, Dave and Chrissy returned the kids. I hugged Chrissy for a long time, even longer than I did Katie and Sam. Somehow, I had to say sorry and thank you all at once.

"The last time I saw you, you were a little girl, and now you're going to become a teacher," I said. "Time flies."

Katie and Sam wanted to show Chrissy Lemon and Minty. That left Dave and me smiling uncertainly at each other in the front garden.

Dave was thinner than I remembered him, but there wasn't much of a scar, I was relieved to see: just a thin white line below his Adam's apple, and you had to search for it. He stood there with his hands in his jean pockets as he had every time I'd seen him over the last few months.

"How was Paris?" he asked.

"Oh, it was lovely," I said. "But how are you?"

"All right. Oh, my neck's a bit short, so Chrissy tells me I need to do yoga to stretch it out again. Guess I should have done it years ago when everyone else in London was getting into it."

I laughed. "I'm glad. That you're feeling better, that is."

Dave looked down, then up again. "Mandy? Can we talk? Somewhere private?"

I couldn't say no, not after everything that had happened. So I nodded, and we walked silently through the side gate into the back garden.

"Alec said you decided not to buy the second salon after all," said Dave as I latched the gate. "What happened?"

How could I answer him? Even I didn't know exactly.

"Well, that day in Bath—all of a sudden, I just knew. That I wanted to be a hairdresser. That's what I always wanted. Oh, I'll keep running Luxor, but it's more about doing hair and talking to clients for me. Helping people. One salon's enough."

Dave studied me. "I'm glad. That you know what you want." He paused. "What did Jack say?"

"He was lovely about it. He's disappointed, but he tries to understand. He wants the best for people, you see."

Mostly for something to do, I started walking. Dave walked beside me.

"In fact," I said animatedly, "he's headed to Glasgow on business now. One of my clients is a copywriter, and he's getting work for her amongst his contacts. Sometimes, I think he likes developing people even more than he likes developing property."

Dave laughed. We'd come to the end of the garden, where two rosebushes grew alongside the wall. Rather than turn back, we stood there, facing each other.

"Mandy," he said, "I've been trying to talk to you—really talk—for months. It seemed like you weren't willing to listen, and I can't blame you, not after everything I put you through. And just before my operation, I gave up hope.

"But when Chrissy said you rang, I started hoping. Especially when she said you asked her to call you as soon as the surgeons were done. And then after my surgery, you asked her to give me—to give me your love.

"But I told myself that was my—the Mandy I'd always known, always looking out for people even when they didn't deserve it. So can I talk to you now?"

I couldn't speak; a lump was in my throat. So I nodded.

He took a deep breath. "Mandy, I know I wasn't all I should be when we were married. Far from it. But you're the only woman I've ever loved. I can't give you what Jack can give you—even with the income from Kodkod, I can't give you what I could twelve years ago. But I need you, and—and I love you, Manda. There, I've said it."

He held out his hand tentatively as though he wanted a rose, but feared a thorn.

I knew his hand like, well, the back of my own. His pinkie was a little crooked. On his ring finger was a white line, a scar from the time he'd burnt his hand on a hob when he was a boy. The fingernails were clean, but clipped haphazardly as though he were in a hurry.

But it was enough. I took it.

Acknowledgements

Mandy and the Pharaohs began as idle speculation. I never intended to write a sequel to *Elsie and the Lynx*, but one day, I started imagining how Mandy and Elsie's friendship might continue. That led me to consider how their lives—and marriages—might evolve as they entered their thirties and the seventies turned into the eighties. The trajectory of the male musicians, the former members of Serval, bewildered by the rise of synth pop, adrift in a Britain beset by income inequality and unemployment, seemed a fitting backdrop for Mandy's story.

To write *Mandy and the Pharaohs*, I read approximately 850 words on Eighties Britain: Graham Stewart's *Bang: A History of Britain in the 1980s* and Alwyn W. Turner's *Rejoice! Rejoice!: Britain in the 1980s*. Together, the books gave me a firm background on the Falklands War, the 1984-1985 Miners' Strike, Margaret Thatcher's cabinet, and all sorts of momentous events and figures that my characters seldom, if ever, mention.

Hunting down details of daily life in the decade proved more challenging. Fortunately, Nicola Herbert of the Marks and Spencer archive not only answered my query about Marks and Sparks locations and departments in the period, but helped me access the department store's excellent archive, a veritable treasure trove for anyone interested in how ordinary Britons shopped and dressed during those years. Once again, Francesca Watson of Cats Protection proved an invaluable source, patiently answering my queries about cat care in the 1980s. I am also indebted to Georgina Brown, Hayley Lawrence, Naomi Mattingly, Miles Taylor, and especially Sarah McCartney for sharing their memories of the decade. Sarah, I am astonished by your ability to recall arcane details about hair salons, newspapers, and colloquialisms. You really do notice and remember everything. In my last book, I neglected to thank Andrew Sanders for telling me "summat" about Yorkshire expressions and for being so supportive of my work over the years. I am also grateful to him and to Rebecca Sanders for introducing me to Betty's of York.

I am especially thankful for my brilliant team. Once again, I was privileged to work with proofreader Molly Spain, designer Shirley Tran, and illustrator Simon Reid. I damn well hope someone judges this book by its cover! Thanks also to Lori Puterbaugh and Lisa Hedicker for lending their artistic acumen to the project. G.T. Lamord provided valuable feedback on the book's first few chapters, while Dolores Dahm offered encouragement throughout the writing process. Mom, you are the reason I write.

About the author

Dora Campbell writes romances with wry heroines, roguish heroes, and imperfect but, she hopes, perfectly satisfying happily-ever-afters. When Dora's not writing, she's reading about British history, volunteering at her local animal shelter, or indulging in dark chocolate. She shares a Vermont farmhouse with a squeaky torbie cat.